VANITY AND VAMPYRES

MANNERS AND MONSTERS BOOK 4

TILLY WALLACE

Version 18.10.20

Print ISBN: 978-0-473-55073-8

Published by Ribbonwood Press

www.ribbonwoodpress.com

To be the first to hear about Tilly's new releases, sign up at:

www.tillywallace.com/newsletter

LATE MAY, 1816. Westbourne Green.

"I AM MARRIED TO A HELLHOUND," Hannah announced upon entering the library.

She strode across the Persian carpet and kissed her mother's proffered linen-covered cheek, before claiming her customary spot on the window seat. Hannah and Wycliff had returned the previous evening from their rather eventful stay at the Pennicott estate in the country. Since her mother had been ensconced in her turret, Hannah had been unable to interrogate the mage and had to wait until morning.

"I am glad you have returned to us, safe and well. Now, did you uncover the information about your husband's condition for yourself, or did Wycliff find a dollop of that common sense he so lauds and tell you?" Seraphina—Lady Miles—glanced up from her work.

The desk's large surface was covered in letters and small notes, as though she created a patchwork from the information they contained.

Hannah let loose a sigh. Of course he hadn't told her. The man held his secrets tighter than an oyster hiding a pearl. "I pieced together the clues. Including scorched paw prints outside our window and the fact that my husband sprouts smoky fur when his hackles are up." Hannah picked up a cushion and ran her fingers through the tassels. She recalled the tingling sensation when she'd stroked the phantom fur that had erupted along Wycliff's bare spine.

"I did advise him that such secrets wouldn't stay buried for ever, no matter how much he might wish it." Seraphina set down her silver pen and the paper, and turned her bathchair.

Hannah continued to torment the fringe on the cushion, until Lady Miles waved a hand and it tugged itself free of her grip to settle on the other side of the window seat. Straightening her shoulders, she faced her mother. How she wished she could peer into her blue eyes instead of at the cream linen that concealed them. "Did you arrange the marriage between us because he is a hellhound, the legendary guardians of the dead?"

Seraphina wheeled herself forward and took Hannah's hands between her cotton-covered ones. Today, Seraphina wore no outer ornamentation to relieve her linen covering, and resembled a marble bust placed in a niche. "No. I consented to the marriage because I know he is a good and loyal man, despite his prickly exterior. His being a hellhound is a potentially interesting development in our search for a cure for the Affliction. Since you are back, you need to tell me all about your stay with the Pennicotts and how you found Mage Tomlin."

Hannah screwed up her face at the mention of the mage—the grandfather of their ward, Timothy. "I did not like him and he was horrid to Timmy. Although I grudgingly admit he had his use in subduing Miss Edith Stewart." While she had only been away for ten days, there was much to tell her mother. Then Hannah's story would need repeating for Lizzie, although her friend would be privy to a somewhat different version.

"And what of your husband? How do you find him upon closer inspection?" Seraphina shook Hannah's hands as though her secrets were apples to be shaken free of their branches.

"I find he is quite good company and entirely tolerable when he stops frowning. Although I am not sure how to proceed." Hannah would keep Wycliff's kiss firmly to herself. The memory warmed her insides and it seemed too precious and delicate to share with anyone else. When she was ready, she might venture to ask Lizzie's expert opinion on the subject. It certainly was not a topic she wished to discuss with her mother. Putting aside Wycliff's kisses, that left his otherworldly nature to consider.

Even Wycliff seemed unsure how to act after their

close time together. He had kept his nose in a book on the return journey and been polite, but distant, when they stopped at the inn for a night. When they returned to Westbourne Green, he had bidden her an awkward good-night (without any attempt at a chaste kiss on her cheek) and then crept to his suite of rooms. Hannah had yet to brave the breakfast room. Interrogating her mother seemed a far greater priority than a cup of hot chocolate and toast.

"I find that when one is on uncertain ground, one day at a time is the best way to proceed," Seraphina said with a chuckle.

"Have you heard what will become of Miss Stewart?" Hannah pulled her thoughts away from the bare chest of Wycliff and to the visage of the lady's companion at the recent house party they'd attended. The one who hid the unthinkable under her turban.

"She is to be interred at the Repository of Forgotten Things until they decide what to do with her. Poor thing. Such a terrible situation, but perhaps she might find some peace now." Seraphina let go of Hannah's hands.

The library door cracked open and little Sheba rushed in with Barnes clinging to her back. The disembodied hand rode the puppy like a monkey on a miniature pony. He leapt down as they crossed the rug and scuttled to the sofa, where he jumped up to perch on the back. Sheba launched herself at Hannah and she picked up the squirming puppy.

"Hello, girl. I did miss you." Once the puppy had

thoroughly licked her face and been cuddled, Hannah set her on her lap so that she might stroke the silken ears. Hannah pointed to Barnes. "I do hope you behaved yourself and didn't terrorise Mary."

"We only had one incident that saw Barnes incarcerated in a birdcage and left dangling from the ceiling for the day. Since then, he has been on his best behaviour. His reading is coming along rather well and he often sits with Timmy during the lad's lessons." Seraphina gathered together a stack of papers and moved them to a corner of her desk. Her actions revealed a portion of a map underneath.

Hannah's mind seemed to bound from idea to idea, rather like the puppy when let loose outside. "Now that we have a hellhound in the family, what do you propose we do with him? Does he change form like a lycanthrope? The fur I saw seemed insubstantial, as though it were made of mist and shadow." Her hand had passed through the red-tinged tips as though she disturbed smoke. Then it had reformed itself.

Seraphina finished shuffling papers and placed her hands in her lap. "In my studies, I have not encountered any other instances of a hellhound shifter. But I rather think those are questions best directed at your husband, who would know more on that subject. Perhaps you can make a start over breakfast?"

Hannah snorted. She had developed a certain sense of bravery around Wycliff, but it wasn't yet substantial enough to ask about his transformation process over chocolate and toast. "I shall work my way up to that topic, Mother."

Setting down the puppy as she stood, Hannah gripped the handles of the bathchair and pushed her mother along the hall to the breakfast room. Sheba trotted at her heels, and then darted ahead to settle on the rug in a sunbeam cast through the window. Barnes scuttled into the room, launched himself at the drapes, and began climbing up to the curtain rod.

Hannah's father sat at the head of the table. Wycliff sat to Sir Hugh's right, where he could angle his chair to stare out the window that overlooked the side garden. Now, he had the addition of a puppy close to his booted feet. Both men rose as the women entered. For a moment, Wycliff's stern features softened as he nodded to Hannah, and he flashed her a smile that made her stomach perform a somersault.

Hannah pushed her mother to her position on her father's left and then took her own seat. She poured a hot chocolate and reached for a piece of toast. Wycliff resumed his seat, holding the newspaper in one hand while he ate with the other.

"When you have a moment, Wycliff, come down to my rooms and we'll take a look at this hole in you. I'm sure Hannah did an excellent job of stitching you up, but we'll see how much longer the stitches need to stay in," Sir Hugh said between mouthfuls of kipper.

Wycliff rolled the shoulder in question. "My wife is rather skilled and handy in a tight spot. I thank you for all you have taught her, Sir Hugh."

He turned to Hannah and she found herself unable to meet the intensity of his black gaze. Instead, she concentrated on her toast. "Do you think I could visit Miss Stewart at the Repository, Papa? While she did a heinous thing, I cannot help but find myself sorry for her situation. Given she is an educated woman, is there perhaps some task she could undertake during her incarceration?"

Her father beamed at her and his bushy eyebrows shot up. "By Jove, there is an idea, Hannah. Most residents of the Repository are not fully in control of their mental faculties. If she were agreeable, there are secretarial duties she could perform. Although it depends what the magistrates decide to do with her. They may yet sentence her to hang."

Hannah touched her throat. How unfair it was that another life might be added to the sad tally resulting from one man's horrific actions.

"I am given to understand that Mage Tomlin wants to cut off the other snake heads in her hair, to see if that reverts her victim Robins to flesh and blood. It seems a likely hypothesis, since the one I severed reverted Stannard to his human form," Wycliff said.

"I assume then that Tomlin did not rustle up a spell to achieve that?" Seraphina murmured over the rim of her empty teacup.

"No. He seemed rather vexed by the task." Wycliff folded the paper and turned his chair so he sat fully at the table rather than to one side. He took two slices of toast and heaped scrambled eggs on top.

A heavy tread heralded the arrival of Frank carrying a silver tray. "Mail," he intoned as he walked to Sir Hugh, pausing only to growl a warning at Barnes, who perched on the curtain rod.

Her father took the mail and waved the hulking man away. "One for you, Lady Wycliff," he said with a smile as he sorted the letters and passed one along to Hannah.

The new title no longer sat uneasily upon her. With each day, and her growing relationship with Wycliff, she became more accustomed to it. Hannah turned the heavy envelope over and recognised the delicate cursive hand—Lizzie.

She lifted the seal with her knife and extracted the sheet within. Rather than finding the usual gossipy missive from her dear friend, Hannah discovered a more formal invitation—her second in a month. Butterflies took up residence in her stomach and she briefly wondered if they were *social* butterflies?

From under half-lidded eyes, she glanced at Wycliff. Her husband was engaged in a similar task of opening and reading his mail. Oh dear, what to do with Lizzie's invitation?

Hannah tormented the edge of the envelope. The contents might not be well received and she was loath to break her new accord with Wycliff. While she shared her husband's aversion to most social events, the invitation was from Lizzie and her loyalty to her friend ran deep. But...a wife was supposed to obey her husband. The idea of going against his wishes so early in their marriage made the butterflies inside her up and flee, only to be replaced by a turbulent ocean.

"Why are you torturing that letter, dearest?" Seraphina asked.

Hannah placed it on the table and dropped her hands to her lap. *Be bold*, she scolded herself as she sat a little straighter in her chair. "It is an invitation to a dinner party. I know Wycliff is not fond of such events and I do not wish to impose upon him by insisting he accompany me."

Wycliff glanced up from the letter in his hands. A frown ploughed a shallow trench across his forehead. "An invitation from whom?"

"The Duke of Harden. It is a dinner in honour of their forthcoming wedding and as his future duchess, it will be Lizzie's first time as hostess at his table. I understand if you do not wish to participate and would rather remain at home. Lizzie is my closest friend and it would be rude of me to decline. I am fully prepared to attend on my own, so you need not inconvenience yourself." Hannah laced her fingers to still the nervous shake. Part of her wanted Wycliff to attend at her side, and conflicting loyalties pulled her in two different directions. Lizzie would win, of course—such was their sisterhood that no man would come between them.

Wycliff made a noise in the back of his throat and the frown filled itself in. "I have no objection to attending. I am somewhat acquainted with the duke and he is a rare type of man."

"What type of man is that?" Hannah heaved a

silent sigh of relief that she didn't have to challenge her marital vows after all. She would have attended regardless of his feelings on the matter. She would never abandon Lizzie on her first foray as a hostess, regardless of how Hannah felt at being inspected during such events. Society waited to dissect the evening with the eagerness of her father with a new type of Unnatural on his laboratory table.

"The duke is the rare sort in possession of a title, a fortune, *and* common sense. I have found most men only possess two out of those three attributes. Naturally, I will take my place beside my wife at the duke's table." Wycliff flicked the paper and returned to his review of the previous day's events.

"Thank you," Hannah murmured, and her heart lightened. Each day they fell more in step with one another.

Then a shadow flowed across her. Would they still be amenable to each other once she probed him to reveal more about his hellhound's nature?

AFTER BREAKFAST, Wycliff descended the narrow, dimly lit steps to Sir Hugh's basement rooms. In his mind, he walked a very different set of stairs. His ancestral home in Dorset, Mireworth, contained a staircase designed to impress visitors. There, the sinuous curve of the double stairs hugged each side of the rounded grand entrance. The wood had once glowed like honey before firelight, and the newel posts were griffins with their wings spread. The stairs met in the middle at the first floor to create a balcony that overlooked the foyer. Above that, a domed lightwell with stained glass depicted another griffin in full flight with a red sunset behind it.

Wycliff worried that damp and woodworm would destroy the imposing staircases. Most of the furniture left in the draughty house had been moved to a drier corner and stored in the corridors, draped in sheets and blankets to protect them. There had been no such insulation he could offer the balustrades and stairs before he had locked the door and left the manor.

An odd sensation wormed its way into Wycliff. Each passing day grew his desire to see his home, and to dirty his hands clearing paddocks and fixing fences. There was another reason, too, deep inside. He wanted to show his bride the estate. But what sort of reaction would the desolate house with its broken windows, crumbling plaster, and leaking roof evoke in Hannah?

Pride burned inside him. He wanted to impress her and, if he admitted it to himself, to create a home that was theirs. Not the roof they shared with her parents. The gothic mansion was roomy and convenient to London, but it would never be his. He longed for the freedom of the wide-open landscape and the beaches that hugged the cliffs.

The season was edging into summer—the perfect time to help Hannah overcome her fear of the ocean and to teach her to swim. Perhaps there were other things he could teach her in Dorset. The memory of the softness of her pressed to him when he kissed her fuelled his hope that their marriage would develop into something far more than *convenient*.

He rapped on the metal door to Sir Hugh's laboratory and then entered. The surgeon turned from the workbench and gestured to the autopsy table.

"If you could remove your shirt and jump up," Sir Hugh said.

Wycliff eyed the cold slab and a shudder worked

down his spine. He'd prefer not to lay himself out on an autopsy table just yet. "I'd rather sit on the stool."

Sir Hugh huffed a soft chuckle. "Fair enough. We don't normally have bodies sitting up and chatting on the slab down here."

Wycliff removed his waistcoat and pulled his shirt over his head before taking a seat.

Sir Hugh peeled back the edge of the spiderweb bandage and examined the wound. "Our girl is far too hard on herself. Hannah makes a neat stitch. This will heal with barely a scar to show for it."

"I have no complaints about her care of me, and found her better than some surgeons I've had the misfortune to encounter." A thread of pride in his wife's abilities wove its way through him. With the exception of Sir Hugh, some battlefield surgeons were no better than butchers. Many a soldier learned how to stitch his own wounds and keep them clean with maggots, to avoid their brutish ministrations.

Sir Hugh pressed on either side of the wound and made a satisfied noise in the back of his throat. "She would have made a fine surgeon if many of my colleagues didn't frown on women studying the medical sciences."

"Hannah would have had your support, though, surely?" Wycliff thought there were many things Hannah could achieve, if she put her mind to it.

"Of course, but it is Hannah who would have had to withstand their barbs and angry words. We could not protect her from that, and it is a heavy burden for one with a gentle soul. In the end, she chose to study away from their judgemental view." The surgeon cut a new strip of bandage and pressed it over the stitches in Wycliff's upper chest.

"Hannah will always have my support, whatever she chooses to study or pursue," Wycliff murmured.

Sir Hugh stared at him for a long moment and then nodded. "I will admit that I had my doubts when Sera told me you'd offered to marry Hannah. I am glad to see those doubts were unfounded."

Wycliff retrieved his shirt and shrugged on his waistcoat. "I know our marriage is not a conventional one, nor did I court your daughter in the ways young ladies expect. But I hope that in the coming years, you and Lady Miles will come to know the depth of my loyalty both to my wife and to her family."

Sir Hugh slapped Wycliff on his uninjured shoulder. "It's not we you have to convince, Wycliff. Treat Hannah right and you'll never hear a word of discontent from me. Nor will Sera need to turn you into some woodland critter."

"I believe life as a toad awaits me if I disappoint your daughter," Wycliff murmured as he took his leave of Sir Hugh.

He walked back up the stairs and fetched the banker's note Lord Pennicott had given him. He tucked the paper into his coat pocket and then patted it twice to check it hadn't magically disappeared. After years of penny-pinching and selling off anything not needed to run the estate, he finally had the means to wrest the manor from the brink of ruin.

Out in the yard, Frank held the reins to the black mare. The sensitive horse nuzzled the monstrous man for treats. As Wycliff checked the girth, Frank slipped the mare a sugar lump and rubbed her forehead.

"Do you likewise slip Mary sugar lumps to gain her affection?" That might go some way to explaining the maid's liking for the monstrous man.

"Pretty. Mary." Frank grinned and there seemed too many teeth in his jaw.

"I suppose she is. If you like nervous types prone to screaming and fainting." Wycliff stopped himself before he asked how Barnes fitted into things. Some aspects of the unfurling relationship between the three were too monstrous to consider. He swung up into the saddle and with a light touch, the mare stepped into an easy canter.

He rode to the banking district and left his mare in a nearby mews. Need quickened his step. Having ruined Pennicott's house party, he didn't want the note rescinded before he cashed it. Although he wondered if the fact that one guest had shot him would earn him a little leeway from the goblin earl.

He conducted his business with a bored banker who spoke in a monotone. Once the funds were secure in his account, Wycliff dispatched a letter he had written earlier to his estate manager, Mr Swift. With his personal business finalised, he retrieved his mare and headed to Whitehall and the offices of the Ministry of Unnaturals.

In Wycliff's short absence, a secretary had been hired to man the front desk. The individual looked up from his paperwork. Large, round glasses covered half his face. Hair in various shades of brown was slicked back from his forehead. A sharp nose ended above thin lips.

"Good day, Lord Wycliff, I am Higgs. Do let me know what tasks you wish me to undertake. I thought as a beginning, I would compile your monthly invoices, if you would leave them in the tray on your desk." The secretary held out a bundle of correspondence.

"Very well. I will review the account before it goes upstairs to Sir Manly for his approval." He had no issue passing on the job of recording his outgoings in the ledger and totting up the columns. Wycliff took the letters tied with green ribbon and wondered what sort of desperation drove a man to take up a position in the new ministry. "You are aware that we deal with matters relating to Unnaturals here? I don't want any fainting or screaming while I am working in my office."

The man still hadn't blinked and his eyes had an unusual amber cast to them. "As a Strigi, I take no issue with working for the Ministry, my lord."

"A Strigi? What is that?" He'd not heard the word before, although it sounded close to *fungi* that grew in the countryside and had a liking for manure.

"I am a man by day and an owl by night." Higgs

finally blinked, an oddly slow closing and opening of both eyes.

Now that the secretary had elaborated, Wycliff saw how the bird overlaid the other man's features. "Is it a shift you control, or one dictated by the fall of night?"

Higgs continued the unnerving stare. "It is mostly brought on by the shift in light at dusk and dawn."

Wycliff grunted. "You won't be working late in winter, then."

"I am a very efficient messenger, my lord, in whichever form I take." The secretary sat taller in his chair and gave the distinct impression of having his feathers ruffled.

"Are you in the register?" Wycliff's gaze drifted to the large ledgers on the shelves behind the secretary. Easily a foot tall, each red leatherbound book held the details of every Unnatural identified in England. Or it would, as Wycliff identified them over the coming years.

A brown eyebrow shot up. "Of course, my lord. My entire family is documented."

"Good." In his role as investigator with the Ministry, he was tasked with cataloguing and numbering the types of Unnaturals in England. The hypocrisy of his actions did not worry him. He would ferret out another man's secret and note it in the ledgers, but the entry of *Hellhound: Wycliff* would never be made in those books if he had his way.

Wycliff walked the short hall to his office, where he tossed the mail to his desk. A new polished wooden tray rested on one corner, with the word *Invoices* written in a neat hand on its label. After a cursory glance to ensure the contents of the modest room were undisturbed since his last time in residence, he left to climb the stairs in search of Sir Manly.

The Ministry occupied a tall and narrow site. Sir Manly had most of the first floor to himself. Wycliff and the secretary shared the ground floor, with what space remained being taken up with a storage area. The top floor tucked up under the roof was, as yet, unoccupied. They also had a basement level that reminded Wycliff of the windowless laboratory built for Sir Hugh. As yet, they had no need to detain dangerous Unnaturals—the Repository of Forgotten Things performed that function.

After a perfunctory meeting with Sir Manly that ended with his superior waving a hand and telling him to carry on as usual, Wycliff decided to take some time for himself. Back on the street and chasing an impulse, he headed toward a little lane populated by bookstores. He glanced at windows while ideas swirled in his mind. He would purchase a book for Hannah.

One store had a range of anatomy books, but Hannah had ample access to those in her father's collection.

Another shop had a colourful display, complete with a suspended parasol and gauzy pink silk scarves, to highlight its display of romantic novels. He snorted and stepped a little faster past that one.

The next shop announced itself as MORRISON'S—

Purveyors of Rare and Unusual Tomes. That sounded more like the sort of bookstore he sought. Wycliff cracked open the door and the bell tinkled as he entered. Immediately on stepping over the threshold, he sneezed. The air was stale like a centuries-old tomb with no visitors to stir up eddies.

Bookcases ran from floor to ceiling and marched in neat rows away from the door on the right-hand side. The left-hand side of the store had a counter running halfway along the wall and two comfortable armchairs placed in front of a tiny fireplace. Candles flickered in wall sconces and lit the narrow shelves.

He wandered down the first row and stared at spines, pulling out volumes that appealed because of the colour or typography, rather than by title. He had offered no wedding present to his wife, and his churlishness now rubbed at him. The amount loaned him by the earl was sufficient for the breeding stock he wished to acquire, but there would be a small sum left over that would allow for a modest purchase for his bride.

He remembered Hannah's delight when he'd found the book about the Fae court and, while it seemed a silly sentiment, he wished to bring such a smile to her face again. Perhaps she would be so moved as to kiss him. Recalling the feel of her in his arms made the blood heat in his veins.

"May I help you, my lord?" a quiet voice enquired. "I am Morrison, the proprietor." Short and of ample proportions, the man's eyes squinted against the dim light behind tarnished spectacles. He possessed a tiny nose and a round face surrounded by sleek brown hair. The entire effect was that of a mole, if one wore a tweed suit and owned a bookstore.

Wycliff wondered what topics would interest Hannah. He knew one and could guess at another. Now that she knew of his particular curse, her mind would conjure up a thousand questions that he needed to steel himself for when she peppered him with them. He thought she would have tackled him on the return journey, but had appeared content to read her book and leave him to his thoughts. "I'm looking for books on Unnaturals and other creatures. The Fae are a particular area of interest."

The odd little man sucked in a breath. "Very hard to find books on the Fae. The barrier between our realms does not allow the written word to pass through. Those who have tried have found they clutch only blank pages."

Wycliff grunted. How then did Lord Pennicott possess such a volume? Or had it been written this side of the fairy realm? "I assume then that they do not send letters?"

The man's shoulders heaved in silent laughter. "Very good, my lord. No, they do not. Messengers are used on the rare occasions the Fae have something to say to us. I hear they only speak to kings and mages. What few books exist about them were written by a human hand after they returned from that realm."

Wycliff considered himself fortunate that he had found one such book for Hannah. "What about books on lesser-known creatures tied to mythology, such as hellhounds or stryx?"

"Hellhounds?" Morrison's eyebrows shot up, but his small eyes remained closed against the candlelight. "One of the most fearsome creatures of legend. While many types of Unnaturals walk our streets, just as many will only be found in the pages of these volumes." He gestured to the shelves with a hand that bore short black nails that tapered to a point.

"Anything on the more obscure creatures might suffice." Having determined to buy a book for Hannah, Wycliff wanted to hunt down a volume she couldn't find elsewhere.

The little man trotted along the rows, muttering under his breath. Wycliff followed at a leisurely pace. His longer stride easily kept up with that of the shorter man. He wondered if Morrison was some sort of mole shifter, or if an accident of either parentage or birth had distorted his form to resemble a blind tunnelling creature. He made a mental note to check the ledgers on his return to Whitehall.

They stopped and Mr Morrison wheeled along the ladder and flicked the lock. With much huffing and puffing, he climbed up to Wycliff's shoulder height and then beyond. "I have a volume on demons with a particular affinity to Hades and the afterlife. I do believe it has quite an extensive chapter on hellhounds, if that would be of interest to my lord?"

"Yes. That may be satisfactory." A cursory glance would tell him if the book knew something on that subject or was a waste of his money and Hannah's time.

"Ah. Here it is. Riverlea's *Daemonology.*" Morrison plucked out a volume with his blackened nails and tucked it against his chest as he descended the ladder. At the bottom, he presented the book to Wycliff with a bow.

He took the squat, almost square volume with its thick, black-rimmed pages. It rested heavily in his hand. Wycliff flicked it open and scanned the contents and then, controlling his excitement, thumbed through to the section that interested him. He sucked in a breath at the brightly painted plate that confronted him. His heart thudded and he nearly threw the book along the row.

One of the creatures who had slaughtered his men, bit into his neck, and chained his soul in Hell stared back at him. The eyes glowed red and the artist had managed to capture the smoky texture of the black fur with its red tips.

"Yes. This will do." With great effort, he stopped the tremor that wanted to crawl along his arm.

The owner chatted pleasantly as he led the way to the counter, but Wycliff never heard a word. Deep, rancid breaths echoed in his ears as his mind tumbled back through time.

"My lord, is everything all right?" A cool nail snagged on the fabric of Wycliff's sleeve and hauled him out of the nightmare in his mind.

"Yes. Perfectly," he muttered.

The bookshop owner had wrapped a sheet of brown paper around the black book and then tied it with a length of blood-red ribbon. He held out the offering with an expectant look.

Wycliff handed over more coins than he'd ever thought a book would cost. Yet he would consider it a worthwhile investment if it raised him a little higher in Hannah's affections.

THE NEXT DAY, Hannah spent her morning being followed around the house by Sheba and Barnes. It seemed that both puppy and disembodied limb had missed her. Her husband, by contrast, was conspicuous by his absence. He had returned home late the previous night and had a tray sent to his room.

After their enforced intimacy, Hannah discovered that she missed Wycliff's quiet company and thoughtful conversation. A boisterous puppy and a silent hand weren't the same.

"How are you feeling, Barnes? You do seem in rude health," Hannah asked as they walked down the hall to the library.

The hand retained a pink flush to his skin. The stitches her father had made long ago to close the wound over the wrist had healed with no signs of scarring or raised tissue. Unlike other Afflicted who decayed without their required sustenance, Barnes had remained as lively and vigorous as ever. Albeit without the rest of his body.

Barnes ran along the carpet, leapt into the air, turned a somersault, and on landing, bowed.

Hannah laughed at his antics. "I take that to mean you are feeling rather well."

The puppy treated him somewhat like a toy, and occasionally grabbed the hand in her mouth to abscond with him. Today, she snuffled at him and licked the upright end of the wrist. Barnes wriggled in what looked to be an approximation of laughter.

"Sheba, don't chew on Barnes—it's not considered polite," Hannah gently scolded the puppy. The last thing she wanted was for the Affliction to pass to the spaniel through ingesting a particle of the tainted limb.

Hannah and her father had made no progress in deciphering Lord Dunkeith's notes about the liquid in which both Barnes and Frank had been immersed. They had tried various formulations over the preceding weeks, but any deceased limb they dropped into the vat remained deceased, and more disappointing—lifeless. Hannah suspected the root cause was the use of Afflicted body parts. They had yet to approach the cursed women to ask for volunteers to bathe in the foul-smelling concoction, while her mother brought down a lightning strike to electrify the liquid.

Hannah decided to clear her mind of that problem by tackling another—hellhounds. Some months ago, when Hannah asked her mother why she had insisted Wycliff be invited to Lizzie's engagement party,

Seraphina had intimated that he had some as yet unclear role to play in their quest. Armed with the knowledge of his true nature, Hannah was determined to discover if there was some practical way a hellhound could wrest the cursed women back from death. After all, if the beast could drag a soul to Hell, could it not act in reverse and retrieve one?

In the library, Hannah stood before the wall of books and stared at the mosaic made from the myriad sizes and colours. Which of the thousands of volumes might aid her study? She considered the wider subject matter under which her husband's kind might fall, and decided the best place to start would be treatises on demons. She scanned the spines and murmured titles under her breath as she searched.

Time passed as she wondered how, given that she was surrounded by thousands of books, she couldn't find anything on one particular topic. Apparently, the family's extensive library possessed only one solitary book that mentioned the topic, and her mother had loaned it to Wycliff. Hannah had almost decided to give up her search and seek him out to borrow the book when, as though summoned by her thoughts, the door opened and her husband entered.

"I had hoped to find you here." He clutched a parcel in his hands, wrapped in paper. "When I was in London yesterday, I took the liberty of purchasing a small gift for you." Rather than giving her the thing, though, he held it tighter and a worry line creased his brow.

"A gift? For me? You did not need to do that." Her heart leapt at such a gesture. Day by day, their interactions nourished the hope burning inside her. She discovered that in her presence, the tension eased from his shoulders. The easy smile Wycliff flashed on seeing her in the mornings quite stole her breath.

His fingers wound in the red ribbon. "I did not give you a bridal gift and I wished to remedy the situation. I hope this will be acceptable to you." He held out the parcel and his dark gaze darted around the room as though he were considering a quick escape. He did have a propensity for leaping through windows, but the narrow ones over the window seat only opened to allow fresh air *in*, not absconding husbands *out*.

Hannah took the object and tugged on the ribbon. It fell away and she unwrapped the paper to find a fat black book. "Riverlea's *Daemonology*," she murmured as she traced the plain gold title with a fingertip.

She flicked through the volume, with its intricate paintings of fearsome beasts. Her hand stopped as one page revealed the image of a hellhound. She bit back a startled gasp. The creature's eyes were a luminous red and seemed to bore through her soul from the page. Its body shimmered with a heat haze rising off the fire-tipped black fur. Drool leaked from between its lethal jaws and stretched toward the ground like a stalactite made of lava.

Was this really what Wycliff looked like in that form? Any idea of his resembling an overly large and friendly black dog fled from her thoughts. Hannah closed the book before the illustration pulled her soul into the pages. Given the skill and care that had gone into the painting, and the rarity of the subject matter, it must have been a very expensive volume. "Thank you, Wycliff. This is a most generous gift and I cannot imagine what it must have cost you. But...I would not wish it to subtract from the funds available for your breeding stock."

His shoulders tensed and he worked his jaw. Had she insulted him by suggesting he should be buying sheep, not unusual books for her?

"There are some things that, while intangible, are still worthy of investment. I consider the money well spent on the book if it pleases you, and perhaps raises me a fraction in your esteem." He placed his hands behind his back and his gaze lowered to the book she held.

She clutched the volume to her chest. He had found her a most thoughtful and considerate gift. "Thank you. It is marvellous and will aid my studies. You are like a knight of old, on a quest to find me such rare books."

A relieved smile flashed over his features and the lines in his brow softened. "I believe that in days gone by, if a knight performed a task that pleased his lady, he was rewarded with a token of her affection."

Hannah stared at him and tried to discern his meaning. The playful humour that emerged from his serious persona in their quiet moments together completely undid her. He wanted a token of affection?

Her throat went dry as she tried to conjure the bravery to offer him a kiss. Instead, she could only imagine her humiliation if he refused. "Yes, you are quite deserving of such a token. I could perhaps embroider your initials on a handkerchief, or ask Cook's assistance to bake you a cake?"

His full lips twitched and she found herself fixated upon them. "I thought to be so bold as to request a kiss."

Hannah had discovered she rather liked her husband's kisses, but lacked the confidence or skill at flirting to initiate them. She set the book to rest atop the others on a shelf and cleared her throat. "I believe such a favour might be bestowed."

She leaned toward him and when she hesitated, he placed a hand at her nape as his lips descended to meet hers. Hannah rested her palms on his chest and pressed into him. A sigh rolled from her lungs and up her throat as they kissed. Heat spread outward from her stomach to reach her fingertips and toes. His fingers at her neck stroked her bare skin and collided with the feelings aroused internally by the kiss.

What if they didn't stop kissing? Hannah's mind tried to juggle two things at once, but couldn't conjure up what happened next while luxuriating in the extraordinary sensation setting her nerves on fire. Then a bang made her jump and they broke apart.

Wycliff turned to glare at the door as the latch rattled and murmured voices came from behind the wooden panels. The door swung open and her father pushed her mother's bathchair into the library.

"Silly me, I was pulling instead of pushing. That's why the door wouldn't open," Seraphina said over her shoulder.

"Really, Sera, how many years have we lived here, that you today forgot how the door worked?" Sir Hugh had his large hands wrapped around the handles of the chair.

Wycliff cleared his throat and said to Hannah, "If there is any other topic you wish to study, I can return to the store next time I am in London." His dark eyes gleamed.

Hannah would ask for a thousand books if he would demand a kiss for each one—but not with her parents in the room. She pulled the *Daemonology* from its temporary resting place and clutched it to her chest. "I shall keep that in mind, thank you."

"Ah. You are both here—excellent." Seraphina gestured for Sir Hugh to turn the bathchair to face them. "Wycliff, are you game to assist us with an experiment?"

"Of course. What do you require of me?" He adopted the at-ease pose, with hands tucked in the small of his back, as he addressed the mage.

"I need you to summon your other form. Hannah and I believe the Afflicted remain animated because a portion of the soul remains with us. Given hellhounds have some affinity for souls, would you be able to confirm or deny such a theory?" Seraphina placed her hands in her lap.

Wycliff glanced to Hannah before answering. "Yes, I am able to see souls when I am the hound. Do you wish me to do it here, in the library?"

"I thought outside might be best, in case your fiery form starts a blaze. We are rather protective of our books." Humour lit Seraphina's words. "Hugh, would you be so good as to take me to the glade?"

"Of course, my beloved, anything to aid the cause." Sir Hugh wore a large grin as he took charge of the bathchair. He winked at Hannah as he pushed his wife from the room.

Before Hannah could follow her parents, Wycliff caught her arm. Worry had returned to his face and pulled at his dark brows once more. "Are you sure you wish to see this? It might be...frightening. The painting you saw in the book is an accurate depiction, unfortunately."

Hannah placed her hand over his and smiled up at him. "Your outward form, whatever it might be, does not scare me, nor will it affect my opinion of you. I know you will not harm me."

He nodded and gestured for her to precede him out the door.

Sir Hugh pushed the bathchair to the edge of the forest and then picked up his wife. He carried her through the trees, like a groom sweeping his bride over a threshold. The sight made Hannah's heart ache. The love between her parents was displayed in so many everyday small acts of affection. She glanced at Wycliff, stalking the path beside her. Was that why he had requested a kiss for fetching the book? Did he, in his own way, show his affection and seek it from her in return?

Hannah puzzled over the possibility as she followed her parents to the glade. She really did need to visit Lizzie. Only the sister of her heart would be able to help her piece together the romantic clues.

Her father set down the mage in the rose-covered bower and took a seat next to her. Hannah walked to what at first glance appeared to be a sawn-off tree trunk. She hooked a finger into a knot hole and lifted, to reveal a storage chest with blankets and cushions within. Selecting a blanket in hues of green and blue, she spread it over the grass closest to the stream. Then she sat down and tucked her feet under her. With her hands clasped in her lap to steady any tremble, she waited to see the true demon that dwelt inside her husband.

4

WYCLIFF STOOD in the middle of the green grass and stared at his fists. Hannah watched him from her seat by the water and he sent a silent prayer to whoever would answer that her eyes might remain free of revulsion or horror when he changed. Never had he called forth the transformation for an audience, nor in the middle of the day—at least, never voluntarily. In the early days there had been times when rage overcame him and the hound flowed over him. Mercifully, when that happened, he had managed to stalk away to the cover of trees in time, so his fellow soldiers didn't witness the hound and open fire with rifles and cannons.

He closed his eyes and concentrated on the ember that dwelt inside him. He blew upon it until flames flared into life and raced along his limbs. As the hound settled over him like a cloak, he dropped to all fours and shook himself. As Wycliff stepped from one realm to another, the light flared and burned his sensitive eyes. He let out a howl and lowered his head.

"Too bright!" he growled.

An ancient language brushed past his ears and a chill lifted his fur. The searing red behind his closed eyelids dimmed to the red-black of old blood.

"Try again, Wycliff," the mage said.

He cracked one eye open. Black storm clouds blocked out the sun overhead and washed the glade in a preternatural twilight. He sat back on his haunches and surveyed his surroundings with otherworldly eyes. The trees and shrubbery emitted a green mist as they exhaled, tinged with a silver spark of magic. Percy the peacock sat by the water's edge and sparkled as though he were made of metals and precious jewels.

Hannah...glowed. His wife seemed to be painted golden and a gentle yellow light came from her skin. The illumination came from her soul, which warmed her very essence from the inside out and lit her body. Sir Hugh was likewise adorned by a soft, daffodil-yellow glow.

Then Wycliff turned and faced the dead mage. He found two mages regarding him. The cloth-draped torso sat immobile in the shade. Next to her, standing upon two legs, was a tall and elegant woman. Long dark hair, similar to Hannah's, tumbled around the face of Seraphina's soul. Her spirit form was insubstantial and what others would call a ghost, with tree breath filtering through her. A thin silver chain floated from the chest of the standing soul to the torso of the seated Seraphina.

"What do you see, Wycliff?" Both forms spoke at once and an odd echo reverberated through his ears.

His muzzle twitched as he stared from one to the other, not sure which to address. "Your soul is removed from your body and stands beside you. You are connected by a strand that appears to run from torso to torso."

"What would you usually see with a deceased person?" When the dead mage tilted her head, the soul performed the same action.

"A dead body is normally a dead body, with nothing remarkable about it. The departed's soul is separate from their earthly form and is not tethered in this way." The hellhound had no interest in the discarded flesh. He scented the souls that sought to escape their final judgement. On instinct, he padded a step closer to the mage's soul.

Sir Hugh sat next to his wife and recorded their conversation in a notebook. He nodded his head and muttered observations under his breath, his words drifting from his living body as golden fireflies.

"How do you consign a soul to the underworld?" the mage asked. The words emitted from the dead form and the standing soul at the same time.

"A void opens, like a tear in fabric, but there is nothing beyond, only darkness. Voices whisper to me, telling me to feed them the soul. I grab it in my jaws and throw it through. Souls have substance in my teeth, and I can tear them from a form if need be." He had derived a certain amount of satisfaction in tossing the reprobate Stannard's soul to whatever awaited him in Hell. Dunkeith would have suffered the same fate, but he had to remain alive to clear Sir Hugh's name. Ripping a soul from a person would result in instant death.

"Can you retrieve a soul?" Hannah's quiet voice asked.

He glanced at her from under smoky fur eyebrows and heaved a sigh of relief. She appeared more curious than afraid.

Wycliff frowned. He wanted to answer no. Those who dwelt in Hell were there for a reason and the idea of fetching one back had never occurred to him. But as he thought about it, not wanting to do something and being unable to perform the act were two different things. "I don't know. I have never tried."

"If you were to try, how would you journey to the underworld?" Another question from the mage spun around the lush glade in an eerie echo.

He stared at his large front paws as he considered the question. "I don't know. I have no desire ever to go there, even if I could."

The two mages laughed. "The form given to you is from that realm. Are you not curious to seek answers as to why you were turned into this creature, or who controls you?"

He snarled and paced the small clearing. The green mist parted as he moved and reformed around him. "No one controls me."

"Are you so certain of that? Cerberus was the hound of Hades. The Welsh have the spectral hounds of Annwn. In Egyptian mythology, Anubis has his jackals. Throughout the world, every culture has some variant of the same thing—the ruler of the underworld has creatures who do his bidding. What makes you think there is no master whistling for your attention?" As the mage spoke, hounds made of silvery cobwebs appeared and loped alongside him.

Wycliff lunged at the phantom dogs and they dissolved in his jaws. Anger surged along his veins, lifting his hackles, and red tinged his vision. Leaves directly overhead wilted as heat rose from him. He answered to no man, god, or demon.

"Wycliff, I believe Mother wants you to question your origins." Hannah's voice flowed like cool water over his heated form. "She was not starting an argument."

He snapped at a tiny firefly that had floated from Sir Hugh and shook his head when the word *Anubis* contained within it buzzed over his tongue.

The mage waved a hand at him and the soul mimicked the action in perfect time. "No need to get all snarly and distracted. Nor do I want our glade burned to a crisp. There will be a way for you to journey between realms, beyond this void that opens and waits to swallow the souls you collect. Look around you,

Wycliff, with your hellhound vision. There will be a path open to you."

"Please try," Hannah echoed her mother's request.

For his wife, he would at least pretend to consider it. He swung his head away in a dismissive fashion and in doing so noticed an empty spot in his vision. He turned back and narrowed his gaze, expecting it to be simply a shadow or trick of the light cast by the trees. His fur shivered as he recognised the same cold and inky darkness as the void. But rather than being shaped like a yawning mouth or a tear in fabric that hung in the air, this was more ribbon-like and lay upon the ground. The track curved between two trees, sucking in all light and giving nothing back.

He trod toward it with his head lowered to the ground, sniffing at the unusual path. His vision picked out nothing—the path simply disappeared into darkness with no hint of where it went or what waited at the end. But a mental tug pulled him along.

As though someone yanked on his leash.

He placed one large paw on the patch of darkness, expecting to fall through into nothingness. Yet something he could not see held his weight. His other foot came down close to the first and the pads registered softness, as though he trod across a rug with a silken pile. He strained with all his senses as he took another step, but wherever the path led, it remained invisible. No scent, sound, or flicker arose from the route.

"Wycliff!" Hannah called from behind him, alarm in her tone.

He spun around. Hannah had risen to her feet, concern pulling at her eyes, and she had one hand on her chest.

He cast one last look at the path and then padded toward her, his head tilted to one side. "What is it?"

Hannah reached out. She hesitated for a moment, then she placed her hand on his head and stroked his ears in the same way she did with the spaniel, except the caress went upward to follow his ears. "You disappeared, as though you stepped through a doorway into a darkened room. I worried that you might disappear and not return."

Wycliff remained still as Hannah grew bolder and ran her hands through his fur. Her eyes widened as the smoky wisps curled around her fingers.

"You will never know what is on the other side, Wycliff, until you follow the path to its end," Seraphina murmured.

"Why do *you* not follow it?" he shot back, not wanting to move as Hannah's hands caused ripples along his sides.

The mage had once told him that her powers had transformed upon her death, and that they now originated from the underworld. What if he followed the path, only to discover she held the end of his leash, while seated upon a throne made of human skulls?

"Perhaps like you, I am not yet ready to confront what I will find." Seraphina curled a hand into a fist and when she released it, sparks of silver spiralled upward and burst through the cloud above to allow a single shaft of sunlight to warm the peacock.

"The answers we seek await us on the other side. Imagine if we found the trapped souls of the Afflicted and returned them to their bodies and restored them to life," Hannah murmured as her fingers massaged along his spine.

In his hellhound form, his shoulder came above Hannah's waist and his eyes were nearly level with hers. Yet she seemed to show no fear, and her touch soothed the last vestiges of his anger.

"But my soul remains here, Hannah. Wycliff says it stands next to me and we are joined by a silver strand. That implies the other Afflicted will also be followed about by their souls." Seraphina tapped her fingers against her thigh. "I feel it is significant that we are tethered to one another, and not separated."

"If your soul were roaming free, you would be fully dead," Wycliff said. Hannah had stopped her caresses and like the spaniel, he nudged her hand to make her restart.

"Well, we have made some progress today," Sir Hugh's loud voice broke through the heavy atmosphere. "We know the soul of an Afflicted is tied to their physical form. Reverend Jones will be most fascinated to learn this, as he originally hypothesised about residual soul animating the deceased."

Hannah stood with one arm resting over Wycliff's back. "If we could find a way to place the soul back into the body, perhaps that would restart the heart and revive them completely?"

The two mages nodded in unison. "We have much to research, Hannah. Why don't you let Wycliff return to his human form now? The neighbours will be worried about the sudden descent of night so early in the day."

"Of course." She stepped away and even though the fires of Hell coursed through his veins, the loss of her nearness chilled his side.

Wycliff grabbed hold of the cool draft and pushed it through his veins. He arched his back as he stood and his vision returned to normal. To fill the awkward silence that followed his transformation, he straightened the cuffs of his shirt.

The remaining physical Seraphina clapped her hands together and the clouds dissolved, allowing sunlight to flood the glade once more. "Shall we expand upon your notes, Hugh?"

Sir Hugh tucked pencil and notebook into his jacket pocket. Then he swept his wife into his arms. "Library or turret?"

"Turret. I always think better in my eyrie." The older couple disappeared along the forest path.

Wycliff glanced at Hannah, unsure of her reaction and whether the hound had interpreted her gentle exploration of his form correctly.

"You were not frightened?" he asked.

She twisted her hands together in the fabric of her

skirt. "I will not lie—your form is frightening to behold. Your eyes blaze as though they contain the fires of Hell. Your fur is made of flames and smoke and you are, quite simply, enormous. I once had a pony who was smaller."

A lump formed in his throat and he swallowed it down. If he could tear the hound from within him and toss it into a bottomless pit, he would. No husband wanted to hear that his wife found any part of him hideous.

Her hand slipped into his and he tightened his grip lest he lose her.

"But within that fire burning in your eyes, I saw your soul. I can never be afraid when I know you are by my side, however fierce you may look." She kept her hand in his as they walked back to the house.

He struggled to understand her lack of fear. Hardened soldiers in his platoon had voided their bowels at the sight of the hellhounds that attacked them. "Why do you have such faith in me? What if I lost control of that creature and struck out at you?"

She reached up and brushed away a curling fern frond. "Because you are an honourable man who vowed to protect me. Your promise is what gives me faith. I choose to believe you, rather than live in fear of the slim possibility of what might happen."

They emerged from the sheltering trees into the courtyard, where the chickens scratched hollows in the dirt to bathe. Hannah's words made Wycliff straighten his spine and raise his face to the sun. Hannah saw something within him that no one else had, and yet she had also seen the very worst of him. Wycliff climbed the stairs to the house. What did the opinion of all of society matter, when one had the good opinion of a marvellous wife?

5

THE NEXT DAY, a loud thumping on the front door
drew Hannah from her studies in the library. "Who is
it, Mary?" she called as she walked down the hall.

For once, the maid had rushed to answer the
summons. Skittish Mary had grown in confidence now
that a seven-foot-tall constructed man hovered behind
her. Seraphina's magic that imbued the house seemed
to allow odd pairings to flourish, rather like the trees
that soared from the earth in the garden.

"It's a man to fetch Sir Hugh, milady," Mary said.

Hannah stopped in the entrance and nodded to the
man standing on the porch.

"Sir Hugh is needed, milady. Lord Burroughs is ill
and his lordship's physician wants a second opinion."
The coachman held out a letter.

Hannah took the sealed letter. "I'll deliver this to
my father immediately."

"I am instructed to wait for either his response or

the gent himself, milady." The man tugged on the wide brim of his hat, which kept the rain from his eyes while he was in charge of the horses.

Wasting no time, Hannah prised open the hidden door in the panelling and took the dark and narrow stairs to her father's basement rooms. She pushed into his workroom and handed over the letter. "A coachman is waiting for you, Papa. Will you be needing your assistant today?"

Sir Hugh slit open the letter and scanned the contents, then he glanced up at Hannah and beamed. "Good idea, Hannah. Could you make sure Timmy is clean and presentable while I fetch my bag?"

"Timmy?" Hannah swallowed the lump in her throat. When she'd referred to her father's assistant she'd meant, well, *her*. Many times over the years she had donned a boy's clothes to accompany her father and had given him her insights.

Her father folded the letter and tucked it into his coat pocket. "Yes. It's time the lad attended these calls with me. He needs to get used to rubbing shoulders with the gentry, without scurrying into a corner like a startled mouse."

"Yes. Of course. I will fetch him directly." Disappointment slowed Hannah's limbs as she walked to the kitchen to find the lad.

He sat at the long pine table with an open book. Barnes perched next to him, tapping words on the page. Cook kept an eye on them and corrected the words the boy got wrong.

"Timmy, Papa wishes you to attend a call with him today. Let's make sure you are clean." Hannah put aside her own feelings, and fetched a bowl of warm water and a cloth. Then she scrubbed the lad's face, neck, and hands.

All the while, he squirmed like a cat soused in a pond and Barnes flicked water at him.

The water and cloth were tinged brown before she was satisfied. Drying her hands on a towel, Hannah fixed a smile to her face and gestured him to the door. "Grab your new jacket and meet Sir Hugh in the entrance. Be quick, mind, the coachman is waiting for you both."

Timmy took off at a trot, while Barnes paced the table. Without the lad to read out the words, his lesson had also come to an end.

"It would seem neither of us are needed today, Barnes." Hannah held out her arm toward the limb, and he hopped onto her hand and climbed to her shoulder.

Returning upstairs, she stood on the porch and watched the horses trot down the road, pulling the carriage back to London. She scolded herself for the tears that pricked behind her eyes. Silly, really. Part of her understood that Timmy would grow into a fine doctor under her father's tutelage. By necessity, that education would include attending patients in their homes. She did not hold a monopoly on assisting her father. Nor did she have the boy's aftermage gift that allowed him to perceive what happened inside a person.

But still, it hurt to be excluded.

A soft nudge at her knee made her look down. Sheba sat beside her, the spaniel gazing up with adoration in her brown eyes. Hannah bent down and stroked the puppy's silken ears and marvelled at the similarity to the feel of Wycliff's smoky fur. Although the hellhound's ears stood tall and erect on his head, like soldiers at attention.

Barnes leapt down from Hannah's shoulder and clambered onto the puppy's back. He hooked one finger into the spaniel's collar to keep his position in the way a person riding bareback might grab a lock of a horse's mane. With her companions at her heel, Hannah returned to the library and her current research topic— hellhounds. Apart from his obvious ability to keep her feet warm, she delved into myth and legends for any ideas as to what else to expect from her husband.

Sheba and Barnes engaged in a game that involved Barnes clutching a pencil as though it were a lance, while the puppy ran at various objects. His tilting skills were surprisingly accurate for an eyeless limb. That threw a new question into her mind. *How does Barnes see?* But Hannah tucked that mystery away for another day, alongside *How does he hear us without ears?*

Hannah dove into Riverlea's *Daemonology*, committing the section about hellhounds to memory. Wycliff had said the picture was an accurate likeness, which she could now confirm. That led her to assume the text was likewise a true account. Tales of fiery beasts that were invulnerable to weapons and whose jaws dripped with liquid fire like the lava spewed from volcanoes. The creatures prowled the countryside searching for souls that had escaped Hell, or those who were deserving of being sent there.

When her mind could take no more, she closed her book and set it on the window seat. Then she turned her attention to her mother, who sat immersed in her own quiet study. "Mother, why have you never heard of a hellhound shifter?"

"I do not know everything, dearest. I suspect there are innumerable Unnatural creatures out there about which we have little to no knowledge." Her mother sat at her desk, reading dispatches concerning mage business. If a mage had something to share with all the other mages in England, they wrote the news on ensorcelled paper and placed it in their rune-covered box. The message then appeared in each magic wielder's box.

The thought of things outside her mother's knowledge didn't reassure Hannah. How many creatures crept from nightmares and scuttled about in the shadows? Or did they stride purposefully across ballroom floors and draw all eyes to them?

Finding no answer to one question, she tried another. "Why do you think the beasts turned Wycliff into one of them when they slaughtered all his men? The soldiers who joined the Highland Wolves were given the choice of whether or not they wanted to aid the war effort by becoming lycanthropes. I am assuming Wycliff was not given any such option."

While their recent stay in the country had seen a warm intimacy spring into life between them, it had not yet evolved to the point of full disclosure about how he had become a hellhound.

"To learn the answer to that, I suspect we will need more information about the night it occurred. But you must exercise patience, Hannah. The man holds his secrets tightly. Give him a little time to loosen his grip upon them." Seraphina spoke without looking up from her task.

Hannah watched Sheba careen around the room with the odd knight on her back. Barnes challenged the fireside set to a battle and scored the first hit against the dangling shovel.

"Blast!" Seraphina tossed a dispatch across the wide desk as though it offended her.

"What is it, Mother?" Hannah rose from the window seat and crossed to her mother's side.

Seraphina turned her bathchair. "A baby boy has been born in France with mage powers."

A birth meant a death, and the transference of power from one mage to another. "Who died?"

"Dupré." The name fell like a stone to the bottom of an empty well.

The mage who had died was the very one who had created the Affliction, who had first assassinated her mother and her friends and then spread the horrid disease to English shores. Hannah's hand went to her chest. "No! How will we force him to reveal the method behind this curse now?"

Seraphina waved her hands in agitation. "We will find a way. Perhaps that is why Wycliff was sent to us. He could locate the mage's soul in Hell and crush him between his jaws or dangle him over some abyss until he tells us how to reverse the Affliction."

Hannah wrapped her arms around her mother. Selfish of her to have hoped they would find a cure before the curse stopped her own heart. This was a blow for all those women who tried to continue with some sort of life. "Yes, we will find a way. You said Wycliff had a role to play in this search and the Fates would not have sent us a hellhound for nothing. You might be right, and he is to become our agent in Hell to find Dupré and end this."

She tried to infuse hope into her words. If one course of enquiry was now closed to them, it freed them up to concentrate on another. Wycliff had seen Seraphina's soul standing next to her, the two forms connected by a silver strand. That was a new clue as to how the deceased remained animated.

Seraphina patted Hannah's hair. "We will find a way, my child. I am determined to see you fully restored to health so that you might live a long and happy life."

A crash, followed by a yelp, drew Hannah's attention. The fireside set had struck back and the poker fell from its hook to dislodge Barnes and bounce off Sheba.

Hannah reassured the startled puppy and then hung up the poker.

"Perhaps Mother could increase your containment area, Barnes, to allow you and Sheba to play outside when the weather is fine." Currently the limb was confined to the house, but he might like a chance to explore the forest and garden. "As long as you promise not to challenge the chickens to duels." Although they would be far pluckier opponents than an inanimate shovel.

"Since he appears to have learned his lesson where Mary is concerned, I am agreeable to creating a new boundary for him. I can extend it to the perimeter of the garden and forest, but we cannot have him alarming the neighbours. I will do that tonight." Seraphina spoke from by the window.

Then Hannah's mother stilled and dropped her hands to her lap, her head tilted. The posture meant her father had rubbed his mage silver ring and sought to consult with his wife. Seraphina needed to reach out with her power to find a suitable conduit for her voice wherever Sir Hugh stood. She spoke when she found one, a conversation in which Hannah heard only one side.

"I am here, Hugh. What do you require?" Seraphina said. A long silence was followed by, "Of course. I shall send Hannah to tell him immediately." Another pause. "All my love until you return, dearest."

Hannah waited as her mother's mind flew back to her body.

"There is something unusual about the death of Burroughs that requires Wycliff's presence. Would you be so good as to send him along, Hannah?" One hand gestured from the window in the vague direction of Wycliff's study.

"Of course, Mother," Hannah murmured.

She walked to the other end of the hall and pondered the fragility of life. Lord Burroughs had begun the morning ill and slipped from the mortal coil as the day unfolded. Had her father tried to save his lordship, or had he discovered him deceased by the time he and Timmy reached the house?

Hannah rapped on the door to her husband's study, where Wycliff split his time between their home and his official office in Whitehall. At the call of "Enter," she pushed it open. "Mother received word from Papa. He requires your presence at the home of Lord Burroughs. Apparently, there is an unusual aspect to his death." Hannah laced her hands in front of her.

Wycliff stood and grabbed his coat from the back of his chair. He shoved his arms through the sleeves and asked, "Did he elaborate on what?"

"No." She tightened her fingers around each other. It was as well her father had taken Timmy. The boy would have a unique insight to offer as to what had snuffed out his lordship's life.

Wycliff buttoned his coat and then reached for his top hat, pushing it down on his unruly hair. He flashed her a smile. "I shall fully inform you of events upon my return." Then he kissed her cheek before dashing out the door.

Hannah placed one hand on the side of her face. A quick kiss was no real compensation for being left behind. Again.

"Right then—no point in spending all day moping about it. I have plenty to do." Hannah glanced around her husband's study and then closed the door on her way out.

There was one very important thing that required her attention—Lizzie's wedding day. Her mother had almost finished the magical elements, and Hannah needed to ensure their correct placement in church and ballroom. She was working on a detailed plan of both venues. Excitement stirred inside her. She had assisted her mother in designing the grand surprise and couldn't wait to see the reaction of all the wedding guests and most importantly, the happy couple.

Hannah vowed that Lizzie would have the most spectacular fairy-tale wedding ever seen in London. Nothing would mar her marvellous day, and horrible murders such as those that had ruined her engagement party would not be tolerated!

6

Wycliff trotted through the house and found the stables deserted, so he saddled his mare himself. There was no sign of Frank, who probably lurked in the kitchen to spend time with Mary. Yesterday, the man had clutched a bunch of wildflowers in his enormous fist. Wycliff chuckled to himself as he tightened the girth. He had expected the household to scream in horror at the constructed man. Instead, they swallowed their innermost reservations and allowed Frank's actions to form the basis of their opinions.

Although it probably helped that Frank displayed his gentle soul and cowered before the puppy. When Wycliff had encountered the furrowed brows and uncertain glances of society, he had chosen a different course. He damned well went out of his way to confirm their low opinion by being rude and disrespectful. Should he have picked flowers instead and curried their favour?

He snorted at the idea of tugging his forelock, and the mare flinched as though he had turned into a fire-breathing dragon.

"Sorry, girl." He patted the horse as he put his boot in the stirrup.

Once on the main road, he gave the mare her head and let his thoughts drift over the countryside as he rode toward London. More and more, he found himself contemplating the inky path that his hellhound self had discovered winding through the trees. If he followed it, what would he find at the end? The ruler of Hell holding the end of his chain, a torturous eternity he could never escape, or a way to reunite the Afflicted with their detached souls?

One face in particular floated before him, one with a warm, intelligent gaze and a waterfall of hair that made his hands itch to have it run over his palms. His hands tightened on the reins. He was no coward and would face his demons if it saved Hannah before her heart stopped. But first he needed to ensure her future, in case he never returned from the path to the underworld.

Wycliff rode to a smart address and left his horse in the mews behind the house. He rapped on the front door, which was opened promptly by a weary-looking butler.

"I am Wycliff. Sir Hugh summoned me about Burroughs' death," he said as he stepped over the threshold and stripped off his gloves to shove them into his hat, before handing the lot over.

"Of course, my lord. If you would follow me, please." The butler passed the hat and gloves to a nearby footman and then took slow, measured steps up the stairs and along a corridor. The butler knocked on a door before pushing it open. He didn't enter and hastily closed the door once Wycliff crossed the threshold.

Wycliff stopped and surveyed a bedchamber decorated in masculine hues of deep green and grey. Opposite the door stood a magnificent sleigh bed of a dark polished wood, with a sinuous curve to the footboard. A tall, wide wardrobe dominated an adjacent wall, with a mirror inset in the middle panel that reflected the unmoving occupant of the bed.

Sir Hugh stood near its foot and waved him closer. "Ah, Wycliff. Thought you might want to see this. Doctor Chartwell did the right thing in summoning me."

The doctor nodded from his position to one side. A man of middling years, with thinning hair and an expanding middle, he packed away a potion bottle in his black case.

Lord Burroughs lay with his hands crossed over blankets pulled up to his chest. Of an age similar to Wycliff, they had passed each other at a few social events over the years. Lord Peterson Burroughs had curly hair of light brown, and a rectangular face with a distinctive dimple in his chin. The skin was pulled taut over his cheekbones. His arms seemed thin under the linen of his nightshirt, and where the garment pulled to one side at his neck, it revealed a collarbone that jutted out starkly against pale grey skin. He had the look of someone who had lain sick and wasted away over a prolonged period.

Wycliff approached the bed and considered the man's countenance. "I met him on a few occasions, but remember him as a more robust chap. What about his death warrants my investigation?"

Sir Hugh glanced up at the doctor across from them, then leaned in closer to Wycliff as though he imparted a great secret. "A somewhat unusual death with symptoms that don't immediately match any disease either Doctor Chartwell or I are familiar with. Apparently, Burroughs fell ill a month ago. He rallied for a time, but in his mother's words, faded away before her eyes. He became increasingly weak and wan, with only short bursts of vigour. Two nights ago, he took to his bed. Doctor Chartwell here was stumped, and so summoned me for a second opinion. Poor chap died while I was taking off my overcoat."

"I initially suspected pneumonia, but his condition did not fit that disease," Doctor Chartwell spoke up, having finished packing his bag.

"Many people sicken and die while physicians are unable to save them. I'm not seeing anything unusual in that to warrant my presence." Nature offered many diseases that struck down the healthy as often as the old or weak. Perhaps the reason Sir Hugh didn't recognise it was because it was not supernatural, merely a more obscure illness.

"Timmy attended with me and he has an interesting finding to share. Come here and tell Wycliff, Timmy." Sir Hugh gestured to a corner of the room.

The lad hung back, almost hidden by the wingback chair by the fire. He stepped forward on command and halted in the centre of the rug. He cast his eyes downward, still unable to look Wycliff in the face. "He's dried up, my lord."

"Dried up?" What an odd choice of words. Wycliff frowned at the boy, wondering if he meant something else.

The lad's gift was still uncertain as he learned not only how to control it, but the basic anatomy needed to understand what it revealed to him about a person's health, or lack thereof.

"Yes, my lord. Dried up like a stream does in a drought." The boy dared a glance at the investigator.

"Does the lad mean Burroughs has been squeezed dry of blood?" Wycliff returned his attention to the body while he waited for Sir Hugh to elaborate. If the man had bled out, the room should have been covered in the stuff. But the sheets and floor looked pristine. Unless they had been freshly cleaned and scrubbed.

"Yes, that's exactly what the lad means." Sir Hugh pulled the blankets down to the dead man's middle and then unlaced the nightshirt to expose a sunken chest. "I undertook a careful inspection of Lord Burroughs and found this." He gestured to a mark above the man's left nipple.

Wycliff leaned closer and found two small puncture wounds approximately two inches apart. He stood and met Sir Hugh's worried eyes. He knew of only one creature that left such a mark and that possessed an appetite for blood. "Vampyre?"

Sir Hugh nodded and then rubbed a hand over the back of his neck. "As you know, the French set them upon our men. Not a particularly effective weapon given their dislike of rain. They also mainly tore with their teeth like rabid dogs. Makes one hell of a mess. But I did see a few who fed more carefully, and they made such a mark as this. It would also explain why Timmy likens him to a stream in a drought. The poor man has had the blood drained from his veins."

"Even if someone had moved him while under my care, he does not have any other wound that would have caused such a monumental blood loss." Chartwell spread his hands.

"If he fell ill a month ago, would it have taken this long for him to die from the blood loss?" Wycliff had no direct experience with the undead creatures, apart from trying to kill one on the battlefield. Could they control their appetites and treat a man as a walking larder, only dining as they required until the cupboard was bare?

Sir Hugh lifted a shoulder. "It is possible that the creature may have fed from him over a period of time, until he reached the point where there was nothing left inside him. I will confirm with Seraphina, as she will know more of their habits. An autopsy will confirm Timmy's findings, I am sure."

A vampyre loose in London? Wycliff let out a sigh. That would be like hunting a needle in a haystack. "Is Burroughs likely to arise as one of the undead?" One vampyre was bad enough—he didn't need a plague of the fops traipsing about London, supping on the residents, and moaning about how the damp made their lace cuffs droop.

Sir Hugh glanced at his young assistant and cleared his throat before continuing. No doubt measuring how much to say in front of the lad. "Rather like lycanthropes, there is a particular process that is required to turn a person into one of their number. The creation of a new vampyre requires the exchange of blood. The victim is drained and then filled by feeding from their sire."

Wycliff's upper lip wrinkled. Perhaps he should give thanks the hellhound had only bitten him and let its poisoned saliva enter his veins. It hadn't asked him to sink his teeth into it and have a nibble in exchange.

"Naturally I shall take precautions, just in case. In vampyres, the liver is the organ of regeneration that allows them to remain ambulatory and defeat decay. Once I remove that organ, he will be unable to rise or to regenerate." Sir Hugh re-laced the deceased man's shirt and pulled up the blankets as he spoke.

Wycliff stared at the victim, sucked dry of his life force. He had better start his investigation, and try to pinpoint how the man had become dinner for an undead creature. "I'll leave you gentlemen to deal with his physical remains. I shall speak to his family and find out where he had been prior to falling ill and who visited him in the last day."

He left the bedroom to find a footman waiting in the hall. "Take me to Lady Burroughs," he instructed and waved the man on.

Lord Burroughs' mother was lodged in her room, where she had taken a dose of laudanum to calm her hysterics. The woman had now lost both her husband and son in the span of less than a year and the toll had proved too much for her mind.

Wycliff took one look at the woman and knew no sensible answers would be forthcoming. He turned to the footman. "Are there any other family members in residence?"

The man wilted under Wycliff's stare. "No, my lord. His lordship has a younger brother, who is at Cambridge. Word has been sent for him to come home most urgently."

From his pocket, Wycliff extracted a small note-book and jotted down the details. "Can you remember when Lord Burroughs first became ill?"

"No, my lord. But his lordship's valet would remember, if you would care to wait while I fetch him?" The footman showed Wycliff to the front parlour and then hurried away to find the valet.

The valet, a young man with a nervous air—rather like a dog kicked often for imagined wrongs—did indeed have a better idea of his employer's comings and goings. "I remember, my lord. It was just on a month ago. There had been some fearful rain and his lordship came home soaked to the skin and so cold he shook. I had to wake the maids to carry up hot water for a bath. Then he slept all the next day and her ladyship worried ever so much about him. We thought he'd caught a chill in the rain, but he did come right for a time after that."

That certainly sounded like the onset of pneumonia. "Do you recall where he had been that night?"

"No, my lord. But his companions might." The valet rattled off four names that all sounded vaguely familiar. And one that was very familiar.

Next, he questioned the butler. "Did anyone call to visit Lord Burroughs in the last few days, since he took to his bed?"

The solemn-looking man shook his head. "Only his mother and the physician, Doctor Chartwell, my lord. We did turn one man away."

"Who?" What individual had been denied entry to visit the sick man?

"His tailor, Daniel Brae. Lord Burroughs had missed a fitting and he wanted final instructions about a suit of clothes. I told him his lordship would send word when he was feeling better." The butler's brows drew further down toward his nose.

Wycliff added the tailor's name to his short list, snapped the notebook shut, and took his leave. Out on the pavement, he regarded the house and considered his options. He could set out immediately to interview Burroughs' friends and, most likely, rouse them from bed. Or he could gather more intelligence about the possible type of murderer first. Forewarned was forearmed, and he didn't want to stumble upon a vampyre to then have to determine how to immobilise it. Removing livers was a messy business and he'd rather not have to fossick about in somebody's belly if he could avoid it.

He decided to return to Westborne Green and set his intelligent wife to learning more about vampyres. Then he would tackle which of Burroughs' friends might have found the man too tasty a treat to resist.

7

Hannah looked up from her seat at her mother's library desk as Wycliff strode across the floor toward her. He moved with such fluid determination that her heart stuttered for a moment. She returned the slender pen to its holder and closed the ledger while she told her heartbeat to settle down.

Wycliff stopped before the desk. "Could I trouble you to research vampyres? There is the possibility that one may be responsible for the death of Lord Burroughs."

"A vampyre?" Hannah could scarce believe that such a creature had taken up residence in London. "Are you sure?"

Wycliff arched one dark brow. "I am open to any and all suggestions as to another method, or creature, that kills its victims by draining them of blood and leaving two deep puncture wounds."

Hannah ran through what creatures and methods

she knew of that removed a person's blood. Not every murder was committed by an Unnatural; an ordinary mortal hand was more often responsible. Butchers hung livestock to drain the blood from them; such a process would also be efficient for the exsanguination of a person. "Father always warned against being too hasty to attribute a cause of death, least that blind you to other possibilities."

"Your father has delivered a preliminary finding of haemorrhagic shock. My concern is the method by which it was brought about. I shall rely on my wife to ensure I am not blinkered to other potential types of murderer." He spoke quietly and a gentle humour infused his words.

Hannah stared at him, took the words at face value, and carried on. "Haemorrhagic shock is where the body shuts down due to both the loss of blood volume to circulate and the oxygen it contains. From memory, Papa once said it is a rather peaceful way to die. Was there significant blood spillage at the scene?"

Wycliff sat on the corner of the desk. "No. The sheets and blankets were spotless. Burroughs seemed remarkably peaceful, as you say, although very gaunt."

Lack of blood wasn't conclusive evidence of a vampyre. Some murderers were fastidious and cleaned a room to remove any trace of the crime they had committed. "Might he possibly have been drained elsewhere and returned to his bed to die?"

"The staff said he was bedridden the last few days and had not left the house. Nor had he received any visitors. I am open to the possibility of a nocturnal visitor who slipped in unnoticed." His long fingers curled around the edge of the desk.

Hannah fixated on his hands and tallied how different they were from those of Barnes. The disembodied hand had developed callouses on his fingertips from using them as feet. "I shall confer with Mother as to other means by which his blood could have been removed, both magical and mundane. Do you require me to assist in your questioning?"

His lips twitched as he considered her offer. "I have his friends to interview, and while I always appreciate your insights, I suspect they will be more forthcoming about their nocturnal antics if a lady is not present."

"Of course." She swallowed her disappointment. She had grown to enjoy their time discussing cases in the carriage, as they travelled from one place to another.

He pushed off the desk and turned to face her fully. "I do require your delicate touch in speaking to Lady Burroughs, though. His mother was quite insensible when I left. Poor woman had dosed herself with laudanum. There is also the man's tailor to speak with, although he was turned away from the house by the butler when his client was too ill to receive him."

She met his dark gaze and a smile touched her lips. "I shall call upon Lady Burroughs tomorrow. In the meantime, I shall research methods of removing the blood from a person."

"Thank you." Wycliff appeared to be on the brink

of saying more, then he merely nodded and turned on his heel.

Hannah tracked her mother to the turret room. "Wycliff says that Lord Burroughs was killed by blood loss. Caused, possibly, by a vampyre."

"A vampyre in London? How unusual. The last one in England meet his end thanks to Sir Ewan Shaw. I suppose it is possible he may have created more of his ilk before his liver was removed. Or there might be others living quiet lives beneath our notice." Seraphina put down the bundle of herbs in her hand and wheeled herself to the bookshelf tucked under the windows.

"I intend to find other means of exsanguination, either natural or magical. What of leeches? Could they drain a person if they were hungry enough?" Hannah sat on the window seat and leaned back against the wall.

"Yes, I suppose leeches could do the job. It would take quite a number of them, though. Ask your father— he will delight in performing the math for you. He will know how much a single leech can consume and can extrapolate that to how many and what time frame would be needed." Seraphina selected a tall and narrow book and placed it in her lap.

"If it's more than two, I suspect the answer is not leeches. Lord Burroughs had two puncture wounds here." Hannah tapped her chest, above her heart.

"Two puncture wounds does sound like a vampyre, but it could also have been another creature with fangs, or something else driven into his chest. Syringes that drained his blood into bottles?" Her mother flicked through the pages of the book. One side appeared to be covered in illustrations, the facing page lines of tight script.

"They would then have needed to be transported away from the scene, and no one was seen entering or leaving his room. Would you climb out a window carrying bottles with several pints of blood in them?" Blast. The more she considered other ideas, the more unlikely or inefficient they seemed.

Her mother selected another book and balanced it on the first, before returning to the workbench. "Was there much blood at the scene?"

"Wycliff says there was none. I thought the victim might have been moved, but again, how? If he was drained to the point of death, he would be a heavy load to carry as the killer clambered up the wall. Or possibly two men could have moved him using the servants' stairs, but that increases the likelihood they would have been seen." Hannah would keep an open mind and gather different scenarios that might fit the sad situation.

THE NEXT DAY, Hannah dressed in a sea-green gown. She thought the muted colour more appropriate for visiting the grieving mother. Her straw bonnet scuttled along the hall to join her and when she captured it, Barnes was underneath.

"Thank you, Barnes," Hannah said as she placed it on her head and tied the ribbons under her chin.

The hand had settled into the household and become more useful as each day passed. Hannah wondered if his previous antics had been his lashing out in frustration and anger. It could not be easy to remember a previous life as a fully-grown man in possession of all his limbs, only to be brought back to life as a mere hand.

Frank harnessed the horses, but Old Jim drove Hannah into London and deposited her on the pavement in front of the Burroughs town house.

"I don't think I will be terribly long, Jim." If Lady Burroughs was still taking laudanum, Hannah might not make it over the threshold. She stared up at the house. She was not expected, and she clutched her embroidered reticule to steady her nerves. Hannah handed the butler her card, newly printed with her title following the wedding, and asked to see the lady of the house. Viscountess or not, she was aware of the enormous breach of social etiquette in a house of mourning.

The butler raised an eyebrow at her and did not invite her in.

Hannah adopted a soft tone to her voice and leaned closer, aware of curtains twitching across the road. "Under normal circumstances I would never disturb Lady Burroughs in her time of grief, but this is at the particular request of my husband, Lord Wycliff, investigator for the Ministry of Unnaturals. As I am sure you are aware, there are delicate aspects to Lord Burroughs' untimely death that I must discuss with his mother."

The butler heaved a sigh and stepped aside. He waved her in. "Of course, Lady Wycliff. We all wish to see the culprit brought to justice. One moment, please." He walked to a set of closed doors to one side and reappeared a long minute later. "Lady Burroughs will see you now."

In the front parlour, Hannah found Lady Burroughs dressed in black and slumped in an armchair. The poor woman had lost both husband and son in less than a year. Red-rimmed eyes peered out at the world from a blotchy face, evidence of the depth of the woman's mourning. A damp handkerchief clutched in one hand, she dabbed at escaping tears.

Hannah nodded a sober greeting as the butler announced her, but the bereft mother barely glanced in her direction. Deciding a direct approach might be best, Hannah chose the cheery blue and yellow striped settee closest to Lady Burroughs.

"I am terribly sorry for your loss, Lady Burroughs, and for this rude interruption," she murmured. She really needed to have a conversation with Wycliff about the proper way of seeking interviews with relatives still coping with their loss. It was one thing if he wanted to maintain his rude reputation, but Hannah preferred to walk a more socially acceptable path.

"He has been murdered, has he not? My darling boy was always in rude good health and now he has been snatched away so cruelly from me. Who would do such a thing? Who?" The last word emerged as a hoot and she leaned forward with wide, unblinking eyes.

Hannah reached out and patted the widow's hand. "Your son suffered an unusual death, and my husband will investigate the circumstances to find the person responsible. It would greatly help if you could tell me when your son first fell ill?"

Lady Burroughs collapsed back against the wing of the chair and closed her eyes as she pressed one hand to her forehead. "A month ago, perhaps? Peterson was out late one night in the rain. His valet said he was nearly frozen solid when he came home and called for a hot bath. He took to his bed for a few days after that. Naturally I sent for the physician, who put it down to a spring cold. It has been so abominably chilly. Is your mother doing anything about that?"

Cold rain continued to ruin the spring and summer. Even on those rare days the sun emerged from behind the clouds, it seemed weakened. Crops sickened across the country and the mages worked to create invisible greenhouses above fields, to ensure crops had the necessary warmth to grow. Hannah's mother had a particular affinity for magic involving weather and, until her death, had taken the lead on such spells.

"Mother offers such assistance as she can." Which meant she worked with those farmers who approached her. Old superstitions ran deep in the countryside and some farmers thought a dead mage akin to a vindictive witch who would ruin their harvest completely and salt the earth after it. "When did you realise your son was not suffering from a spring cold?"

Lady Burroughs dabbed at her eyes and then blew her nose into the overtaxed piece of cambric. "Now that I look back, he didn't seem to have the sniffles or a cough. He slept a great deal and was dreadfully pale, but then seemed to rally."

"Do you recall his activities preceding that first bout of illness? Had he been anywhere new or done anything out of the ordinary?" Hannah steered the conversation in the required direction.

The handkerchief waved through the air. "You know these young men, up to all sorts of things they don't want their mothers to know of."

The man's valet had provided Wycliff with a number of leads and, given their nature, it was little wonder he didn't want his mother to know how often he frequented the gaming hells or the sporting houses.

"What of his downturn this week? Can you recollect if he did anything unusual before it happened, or had any visitors?" Hannah grasped at straws. So far, she had little to relate to Wycliff that might assist his enquiries.

"Not that I can recollect. And he seemed so weak and gaunt. Why, he could scarcely leave his bed to use the chamber pot. I had a footman stationed outside his door in case he required assistance and we heard nothing from his room. Then yesterday morning..." Her voice trailed off and the tears recommenced.

Hannah patted the woman's arm. "I'm so sorry. Did he rouse at all, or say anything before he succumbed?"

A shake of the head as the woman sobbed. One shuddering breath was followed by another, as she sought to compose herself. "I was so worried. You will understand when you have children of your own. I awoke early myself to rush to his room to see if a good night's sleep had aided his recovery. And there was my beautiful boy, looking so peaceful but so dreadfully still. I called for Doctor Chartwell immediately, but nothing would rouse Peterson. Then it was suggested we summon Sir Hugh Miles for a second opinion."

"I'm so sorry my father could not assist." From the discussion she'd had with her father, she understood the poor man had been beyond help by the time he arrived. Hannah fell silent. There was little for her to learn, and her visit had only raked over the hot coals of grief.

Then she remembered one other detail. "When did the tailor call? Mr Brae, is it not?"

Lady Burroughs stared at Hannah for a long moment before replying, as though she hadn't heard the question. "Oh, yes. Peterson missed his appointment and the little man was most eager to finish his commission. When he was informed my son was ill, he toddled off again, so I understand, with his portmanteau under his arm."

"Thank you, Lady Burroughs, for seeing me during this most distressing time." Hannah took her leave and walked out to the carriage.

She hoped Wycliff's enquiries were more productive than hers. But, since she was in London with little else to do, she decided to call upon Daniel Brae, and gave the address to Old Jim before climbing into the carriage.

When she arrived at the shop on its quiet street, Hannah pushed open the door and marvelled at the difference between the atelier of a gentleman's tailor and that of a lady's modiste. The room had dark panelled walls, brass lamps, and leather armchairs such as one might find in a gentlemen's club. One wall held bolts of dark coloured fabrics, suitable for making jackets. An open wardrobe was crammed with smaller folded lengths of silks and satins, both plain and embroidered. A counter covered in glass drew her attention. Underneath, pinned like exotic butterflies, were laces of delicate and extraordinary beauty.

"May I help you, madam?" a soft voice asked from behind.

"Mr Brae?" Hannah asked as she turned, pulling her attention away from the lace.

"Yes." The tailor was shorter than Hannah and with perfectly coiffed blond hair. One curl draped artfully over his forehead and his skin was powdered a rosy hue in the quaint, old-fashioned way of long-ago courtiers. He wore a jacket of deep blue with short lace cuffs and on one wrist, a plush, blue velvet pincushion. Crisp blue eyes regarded her with curiosity. He had a lean figure, perfectly displayed by the exquisite cut of his jacket and breeches.

Hannah couldn't help smiling at the impeccably dressed man. "I am Lady Wycliff and I am assisting my husband in his inquiries into the death of Lord Peterson Burroughs."

"Such a tragedy," the little man murmured. He gestured toward a chair before the fire.

Hannah perched on the edge of the seat. "I am told he had an appointment with you?"

The tailor rearranged the pins in the cushion at his wrist so they formed a neat circle. "Yes. He had ordered a range of new clothing and we were to have the final fittings for a jacket and waistcoat."

Hannah watched the tailor select a pin and wondered how much blood a prick would draw forth. "When did you last see Lord Burroughs?"

"I would need to check my appointment book." He walked to the counter and pulled out a large book from underneath. He flicked it open and ran his finger down a column. "It was over a week ago. The garments were to be finished this week and I was to be paid before delivery." His lips tightened on the last three words.

Hannah tucked away his reaction. Tailors were often last to be paid, nobles preferring to spend their money on their entertainments. "Might I ask about the lace? Your range is remarkable and more beautiful than anything I have seen in any modiste's rooms."

He smiled and revealed perfect white teeth. "I spent some time finding artisans who make the lace to patterns I create. I pride myself on offering the best selection to the most discerning men in society. Not that many wear lace anymore, as it is no longer the fashion."

Hannah walked to the counter, one piece in particular again catching her eye with its strong geometric design. What a shame Wycliff didn't wear lace cuffs. She could imagine it peeking out at his wrists. "I am surprised ladies aren't clamouring to purchase from you. I have not seen its like in any shop."

"Thank you. I have thought of offering a small quantity to a high-quality modiste, as I believe ladies are more reliable in paying their bills than young men." He opened the back of the cabinet and pulled out the tray holding the piece that Hannah had been admiring.

"Not always, I am afraid, since often their husbands control the purse strings. Might I enquire as to the cost of this piece?" Hannah seldom gave in to frivolous impulses. Today, on a whim, she decided to purchase the lace and paid for it immediately. She left clutching the small paper-wrapped parcel and wondered how best to use it. She could decorate a gown of her own, or tuck it away in case one day the opportunity arose to give it to Wycliff.

And, perhaps, seek a token of affection in return?

8

LATER THAT AFTERNOON, Wycliff once more rode for London to pay his not-so-social calls. His first port of call was with the man Burroughs' valet had identified as the deceased's closest friend—Lord Samuel Enderley. The lord was roused from his bed by his valet and Wycliff was shown through to a small sitting room adjacent to the bedchamber. Clad in a robe of orange and red patterned silk cinched at the waist, the man lounged on a chaise with a hand pressed to his forehead. Brown hair curled around his ears and brushed against his unshaven cheeks.

The parlour appeared to double as a dressing room, with clothes strewn over the furniture. One shoe rested in the middle of the floor with no sign of its mate. The faint aroma of stale cigar smoke and perfume hung in the air. Wycliff wrinkled his nose to stop a sneeze. The room needed a good tidying up and an airing, and the fop needed his head plunged into a bucket of cold water.

"What blasted time is it?" Enderley asked of no one in particular.

"Nearly four." Wycliff flicked out the tails of his coat and took a seat. "I need to ask you about Peterson Burroughs."

"What about him? Haven't seen him for a few days now. Dashed rude of him to avoid our company." Enderley swung the tassel at the end of the robe's tie.

"He's dead. When were you last out together?" Wycliff extracted his notebook and pencil.

"Dead?" Enderley sat up and lowered his feet to the floor. The quick movement made him moan and he pressed the heel of his hand to his head. "That's a rude jest to play on a fellow."

Wycliff stared at the fop. Did he look like the sort of person to rouse another man from bed simply to play a jest? "He died yesterday morning. I am told he was with you the night he first fell ill, approximately a month ago."

"Did pneumonia get him? And why are you investigating that? God, it wasn't the cholera, was it?" Enderley laid his hand flat on his forehead and appeared to be taking his own temperature. Then he lowered it to his neck as though he searched for a pulse.

Wycliff exhaled impatiently through his nose. Nattering with the likes of Enderley reminded him why he held such a low opinion of most wastrel lordlings. "There are unusual circumstances concerning his death. Now, tell me about the night he fell ill."

Enderley collapsed against the rolled back of the chaise. "Dead? Life is cruel. Why is it always the young and beautiful who are cut down by the Reaper in their prime?"

Wycliff thought it was usually because they were damned stupid and ran into the Reaper's scythe. Although in this case, the man had been pushed into the afterlife. He tapped his notebook with the pencil. "Where did you go that night?"

"Let me see, what did we get up to the last time I saw him?" he muttered.

The clock over the mantel ticked. A shaft of sunlight crept through the gap in the curtains and across the floor to become a warm hand that caressed Enderley's slipper-clad toes.

"Ah! Now I recall. We usually start our evening at Fletches. We drank and gambled for an hour or so. Then we heard that Baron Medwin had a new performance that night, so we stopped by for a time. He often puts on these puppet shows with rather hilarious stories." As he described the show, he lifted his arms up and down in a pantomime of invisible strings pulling them. "Although they are rather disturbing, they look too lifelike and I wondered if they were kept in a trunk if they misbehaved. When we grew bored, we went to La Perfumeria."

"La Perfumeria?" Wycliff had heard of the place. Contrary to its name, it didn't sell perfume. Or it did after a fashion—amply drizzled over the décolletage of expensive courtesans.

Enderley sat up, his eyes bright and glazed as though alcohol still flowed through his veins. "Yes. Have you been? Quite an extraordinary place, with a range of exotic delights on their menu. They have a woman who is one of those Unnaturals and she is part panther. She will change forms and let you stroke her fur for the right price."

Wycliff arched one eyebrow. "No. I did not know that. Did you two spend time with her?" He scribbled a note to ensure the panther shifter was recorded in the Ministry's ledger of Unnaturals. Along with whatever other *exotic delights* he might find in the establishment.

Enderley snorted. "Hardly. That wasn't Burroughs' taste. After a few drinks we parted company for a time. He to the room of Princess Penelope, I—well, that's not relevant here, is it?"

"Princess Penelope?" The pencil hovered over the page and Wycliff waited for the man to elaborate. Somehow, he doubted she was a genuine princess, although one did find old European royalty in the oddest places.

A sly grin crept over Enderley's face. "Prim and proper Princess Penelope. Personally, I couldn't fathom why you'd pay good coin to try and sidle up to a lump of ice. I can go to any ball and have prissy debutantes turn their backs on me, but Burroughs seemed to enjoy her bite."

"Her bite?" Wycliff leapt on the use of that word, but kept his opinions about the noble's preferences to himself. At least the man paid a courtesan to act the role of reluctant ingenue, rather than dishonouring a young noblewoman.

"Yes. She likes to nibble, that one. You know, leaves those little love marks on a fellow's neck that get him in dashed trouble if he happens to be married, or has a mistress tucked up somewhere." He rubbed a hand over his neck, as though ensuring his skin was free of such marks.

Wycliff grunted. He would have a talk with Princess Penelope about her appetites. If she were known to bite, perhaps she also fed on the men who visited her. He had heard tales that some found a type of pleasure in being used in such a fashion by those particular undead creatures. Women in France were known to bare their breasts to their vampyres, pleading for their bite. "Did you reconvene that evening or go your separate ways?"

Enderley tapped his chin with his forefinger. "We left together. It was raining, wasn't it? I seem to recall getting soaked to the skin as we walked home and traded tales of what we'd got up to. Completely ruined my good blue silk. Had to get Brae to make me another." A wistful look dropped over his lordship's face and gave the impression he missed his waistcoat more than his friend.

Wycliff's hand froze over his notebook. "Daniel Brae? You use the same tailor?"

"Of course. He's the only tailor in London a man *should* use if he wants to be considered well-dressed." Enderley narrowed his gaze to peer at Wycliff's attire. After making a dismissive noise in the back of his throat, he collapsed once more against the chaise.

"Have you heard from Burroughs this week, or did you visit him while he was ill?" Wycliff ignored the slight against his attire. His clothing was perfectly adequate and durable. He made a list of the establishments mentioned and that he would visit as he retraced the dead lord's steps.

"I dashed off a note, enquiring when he would be back in fighting form. I don't think he answered, and I've been far too busy to call on him. Besides, a man doesn't want his peers gazing down on him when he's not looking his best. And he might have given off sick fumes and contaminated me." He waved one elegant hand and turned to stare at the sliver of sky exposed between the curtains. Probably contemplating how to dress should the Reaper pay him a call.

"If you think of anything else, send word to me at the Ministry of Unnaturals." Wycliff tucked the notebook back into his pocket and took his leave. Outside, he studied the short list of names of the remaining associates to tackle: Cecil Thornton, James Stoneleigh, and somewhat surprisingly, Francis, the Duke of Harden.

During Wycliff's calls on the first two lords,

Burroughs' friends both told a variant of the same tale. They'd gone to their favourite gaming hell, Fletches. There, they spent too much money and drank too much, before taking in the entertainment at Baron Medwin's home. The last port of call for the group was also usually La Perfumeria, until they were ready to return to their own beds and sleep until the next afternoon.

When he knocked on the door of the duke's Mayfair residence, the butler informed him that Harden was not at home. Wycliff considered how to tackle him without alarming either Hannah or her close friend if his investigation revealed the duke had paid for unusual favours at La Perfumeria. The dinner party at which he was a guest was not far away, and while that might provide an opportunity to ask a few quiet questions, he'd rather have the matter resolved before then. Hannah wouldn't want the evening tainted by either death or the revelation that Harden liked to sample *exotic delights*. What liberties would a panther shifter allow a patron to take if he dangled a large enough purse? Best not to discover any sordid secrets about the duke at his fiancée's first time as hostess.

Next, Wycliff called at Fletches as they made the rooms ready for the evening's entertainment.

"Can I help you, my lord?" A young man with a mop of fashionably tousled hair asked as he swept the floorboards in the foyer.

"Who is in charge?" Wycliff cast around. He knew

of the gaming hell, but had never frequented it. Men and their money were too easily parted in such places.

"Mr Fletch. You'll find him through there, checking the tables. You can't miss him, my lord." The youth winked and went back to his sweeping.

Wycliff bit back a retort. He could stand in the entrance and try to extract a better description from the lad, or circumvent the process by walking into the next room and asking again. He pushed through the double doors and paused. The gaming room had walls of dark panelling on the bottom and a forest green wallpaper with trees and birds on the top half. Brass chandeliers hung from the ceiling and were decorated with leaves in autumnal tones. Rich rugs in brown hues were scattered over the floorboards. The entire décor gave the effect of being in a secret woodland grotto.

It transpired the lad was right. With one glance at the people in the room, Wycliff made straight for one in particular. The one who possessed the same short stature, bald head, protruding forehead, and pointed ears as Lord Pennicott. Who better to run a gaming hell than a goblin? The bucks who lost their allowances here would find no sympathy in such an owner.

"Mr Fletch, I am Lord Wycliff and I am investigating the death of Lord Peterson Burroughs. I need to ask you a few questions." Wycliff stopped before a table covered in green felt.

The goblin stared at him with such a calculating look in his eye that Wycliff had to resist the urge to check the coin purse in his pocket. A quick grin pulled the goblin's thin lips tight. "Of course." He waved his hand and the other men were dismissed; they seemed to disappear into the painted forest.

"Do you remember the night Lord Burroughs was here, about a month ago?" Wycliff leaned one hip on the table and crossed his arms.

The goblin chuckled and his ears twitched. "No. We are busy here at night and many people come and go. I can tell you how much he lost or won, though. I had heard of his passing and my man will be presenting his chits for payment."

Wycliff grunted. A goblin would keep detailed records down to the last ha'penny that passed through their fingers, but was blind to whom a man drank with, or which woman draped herself around his neck. "Do you recall if he had any disagreements that night?"

Fletch shook his head. "We do not tolerate fighting here and my men are quick to settle any arguments. During the night, I only take occasional strolls around the tables to monitor activities. Otherwise, I stay in my office and the men fetch me if there is an issue. I need to consult my books when a patron asks for credit to be extended." He waved to a wall where leadlight windows obscured the room beyond.

"I'll have the details of his gambling for the last night he was here." Perhaps that might reveal more.

The owner scurried away to his den and flipped through his books. He returned some time later with a sheet of paper bearing a neat list of numbers. "His wins and losses for the night and the amount now due, my lord."

Wycliff scanned the page. Lord Burroughs had modest tastes, judging by his bets. He'd begun the night with a small amount and ended it only a few pounds in debt. "Do men ever make allegations of cheating?" Perhaps the lord had lost a larger purse than was detailed and had taken a disagreement outside.

The goblin's gaze hardened. "Not in my establishment. Anyone caught cheating is banned."

"And the tables are run fairly?" Wycliff murmured and dropped his attention to his nails.

The house always emerged better off than its patrons. Some of the gaming hells let the odds play out; others took matters into their own hands to ensure they always came out ahead. Many a hotheaded buck started a fight when the cards dealt, or the dice rolled, didn't play in his favour.

"The *ton* come here because of my reputation for fairness. A good businessman has no need to *cheat*." He spat the word out as though Wycliff had thrown the greatest insult at him.

He racked his brain for scuttlebutt about the place and couldn't recall ever hearing anything that hinted at such practices. "If you think of anything else, send word to the Ministry of Unnaturals." Wycliff nodded and strolled back through the building.

Afternoon had lengthened into early evening by the time Wycliff left the gaming hell. He stared up at the darkening sky and the gathering threat of rain, and decided enough was enough for the day. He stood under a street lamp to scribble a few last-minute thoughts before retrieving his mare. As he placed his foot in the stirrup, he found a knot of anticipation inside him at the thought of a quiet evening in the drawing room, discussing the investigation with Hannah. The need to seek his wife's opinion drew him home to Westbourne Green.

9

The following morning over breakfast, they again took up the progress, or the lack thereof, in the case. Hannah stared into her hot chocolate as she brought together the physical findings of her father with the answers elicited by Wycliff.

"To all intents and purposes, Lord Burroughs was a fine specimen of health with no other disease evident within his body," she mused out loud.

"Fit as a fiddle, inside and out. Cause of death haemorrhagic shock due to the blood loss. I'll leave it to you two to discover how that was done," her father said as he dished up his breakfast from the sideboard.

"Which leaves us with limited prospects as to how the blood loss occurred." Hannah played the foil in Wycliff's investigation. He focused on finding the vampyre among Lord Burroughs' associates, while she searched for other means to drain a man of his blood.

"I am calling on Baron Medwin today, Hannah, if

you have time to accompany me?" Wycliff asked from across the table.

"Of course. I have heard whispers about him, but ladies do not attend his evenings." Hannah gathered together the scant information she held. Rumours painted him as a pantomime villain complete with cloak and mask. Disfigured in a terrible accident, he hid his appearance. Young nobles flocked to his address for his renowned magical entertainments; she had been curious to see how they compared to the delights her mother crafted.

"Do let me know what you discover, Hannah. He cannot be an aftermage, as no Medwins appear in the genealogies. I am curious about his little shows." Seraphina patted her daughter's arm.

After breakfast, Hannah took Sheba and Barnes out to the forest. Due to his good behaviour, her mother had extended the perimeter that enclosed the disembodied hand, and he seemed rather excited about the new arrangement.

"No scaring Mary or the chickens," she warned him as she set him down on the packed earth.

Puppy and hand scuttled off on some strange adventure, thankfully in the opposite direction from where the chickens scratched among fallen leaves. A muffled bark sounded from the undergrowth as the two embarked on their exploration.

Hannah set off through the trees, touching trunks as she progressed deeper into the shade. Her fingers sought the grooves in wrinkled bark, greeting each as though they were old friends. Percy the peacock cried out and she stopped to allow him to pass, dragging his magnificent train, followed by his harem of dull peahens. When she reached the quiet glade, Hannah sat in her mother's bower and called to mind the day Wycliff had shifted forms. A shiver ran over her skin as she thought of how he had stepped between two trees and disappeared. What awaited him at the end of the phantom path?

How she wished she could accompany him, so he did not travel to the underworld alone, but that would require her to be dead. One hand went to her chest, to find the reassuring steady thrum under her fingertips. Her mother's magic only temporarily halted the curse within her body, and each day she wondered when her time would be cut short.

Snatches of ideas drifted through her mind like dust motes. She plucked a few and wondered how they fit might together. After an hour of silent contemplation, and with the beginnings of a course of action taking form, Hannah walked back to the house.

LATER THAT DAY, Hannah stood on the pavement on the fringes of Soho while Wycliff rapped on a glossy black front door. She clasped her reticule with both hands and pondered whether she ought to ask her mother to craft her a magical one capable of transforming into a large metal shield. There were days she wished the small bag were capable of hiding her, or at least that it concealed some type of useful defensive device.

While they weren't in an undesirable part of London, nor was it quite as fashionable or as respectable an address as she normally frequented. Since she had Wycliff's protection, it wasn't the location that set her nerves on edge. Rather, it was the rumours she recalled Lizzie whispering in her ear about the baron. Unlike some who might be apprehensive about the sight of the man's disfigurement, Hannah swirled with curiosity about the nature and extent of his wounds and what medical cures he sought.

Wycliff spoke to the butler in a quiet tone and the man showed them through to a modest foyer. Muted red and dark grey tiles were laid out under their feet like a giant checkerboard and Hannah wished for markers to play a quick game while the butler conferred with his master.

"Baron Medwin will see you, my lord and lady." The butler possessed a light tone and didn't seem either stern enough or old enough to hold such a position.

As Hannah stepped into the front parlour, a tingle washed over her skin. Instinctively, she reached out and slipped her hand into Wycliff's. He slowed his step. "I tingle," she whispered.

He nodded, understanding the message that her particular sensitivity had detected a magical vibration. Not surprising, really—the baron was known for using magic in his entertainments. She cast around the room to find the source. Perhaps his ensorcelled puppets were nearby.

The room continued the deep red and grey theme, from the drapes to the rugs on the floor, relieved only by a chesterfield suite in a rich brown leather. A spray of flowers sat in a large vase on a side table: blood-red roses stripped of their foliage and nestled among bare twigs.

The baron rose from a chair set before the fire. Of modest height and stature, he wore an outfit in tones of grey as though someone had drawn all the colour from him. It was his face that halted Hannah's feet. Not that he appeared hideous or frightening. That she had prepared herself to find. Instead, the baron possessed the handsome face one often saw gazing down from a fine painting. Hannah was sure that if she peered closely enough, she could see the brush strokes. It was a marvellous enchantment, although it did lack depth. When he turned his head, a thin edge became visible where the painting hovered an inch in front of his real face like a stiff paper mask.

"Lord and Lady Wycliff. To what do I owe this honour?" He bowed and a painted eye rolled sideways to Hannah.

"The death of Lord Burroughs," Wycliff said. "I have questions about the night he came here with his friends."

Baron Medwin gestured to the leather sofa. "Please, be seated and I will ring for tea."

Hannah took the end closest to the fire laid in the

hearth. A chill settled over the room and she wondered why he had not lit the kindling.

Wycliff flicked out his coattails as he sat beside her. "There is no need for the glamour, and I'd rather look you in the eye when we speak."

The painted face turned to Hannah. "I would not distress Lady Wycliff."

Hannah rested one hand on the rolled arm of the sofa. "I assure you, Baron, that despite my appearance I am robust and not given to fits of fainting. I have worked alongside my father, who is a surgeon, for many years and seen much in my short time on this earth."

Medwin returned to his chair and tapped his fingers on the arm for a long moment. The butler arrived carrying a silver tray and set it on the table before them. The porcelain cups had silver rims and a pattern that reminded Hannah of the bare twigs in the vase. She sat forward and turned the handle on the pot toward herself, ready to pour tea.

"Very well," the baron said once his man had left the room.

He reached up and pulled forth a chain that hung under his cravat. At the end of the chain was an amulet, its golden case holding the same painted miniature that overlaid his features. The baron touched a button on the side and the outer casing swung from behind the portrait to snap closed over the image. As the tiny painting was removed from view, the illusion fell from his face as though a sudden rain had washed away the paint.

Hannah placed a hand to her chest, but not for the reasons the baron feared. Some people would stare at his ruined features and recoil in horror. They would form their opinion of him based upon a tragedy that claimed nearly half his face. The left side seemed almost untouched and rather handsome. A bright blue eye regarded her with a steady gaze. The dark brown eyebrow had the perfect arch and lush brown hair tumbled in soft curls around his high cheekbone.

The right side of his face bore stripes of tight pink and white that pulled his skin taut. The right ear had been burned away, the nose ruined, the eyebrow missing entirely. Burns swirled down the side of his neck and disappeared under his shirt collar. The right eye held a murky and muddied gaze. The hair on that side of his head was shorter, coarser, and large parts were missing, exposing patches of scalp.

The baron pushed himself back in the chair. "You stare so intently at me, Lady Wycliff. Is it taking so long to catalogue all the ways in which I horrify you?"

"On the contrary, Baron Medwin. I see nothing that disturbs, apart from imagining the agony you must have endured." Hannah regarded his wounds and saw layers of pain, both in the initial fire that had inflicted the wound and the long period of healing. "The skin appears rather tight and if it troubles you, my mother brews an unguent that gives relief to burns. The oils soothe and soften the skin, and it contains a mild analgesic that provides localised pain relief."

The baron stared at her, one eye narrowed and the

other opened wide—an odd and disconcerting effect, as though two different people looked out at her from one set of features. "You look upon my face and ask if I suffer pain? Are you not horrified?"

Hannah poured the tea for each man and then picked up her own cup. "That you were injured in a terrible accident is horrific, but that does not make the man before me horrifying. Others may judge you based on an accident, but I prefer to observe a person's actions and how they respond to the world around them."

He huffed a gentle laugh and shook his head. "How extraordinary. Although I must remember you married Lord Wycliff here, which says much about your ability to perceive the inner character of a man."

Hannah hid a smile behind the teacup. Closer association with Wycliff did indeed reveal hidden depths that he concealed behind a prickly exterior.

Wycliff glared at the baron, then pulled the notebook from his jacket pocket. "Can you recollect the evening a month ago when Burroughs was here?"

"One evening is much like another. I have a select group of young friends whom I invite when my troupe is ready to perform. Burroughs is one of many nobles who cross my threshold." He waved a hand and then used it to prop up his chin. Turning his face away from the light, he cast the ruined half in shadow so the handsome side regarded Hannah.

"Did he have any altercations while here?" Wycliff asked, ignoring the cup of tea.

The baron shook his head, sliding his chin back and

forth over his knuckles. "Good-natured ribbing, nothing more than what you might expect from a group of young men out for an evening when the wine flows freely."

Wycliff jotted notes in the little book. "What did they do while here?"

The baron smiled, one side of his lush lips tilting upward. "The same as everyone else. They drank, they laughed, they watched the performance."

"With whom did he leave?" Wycliff asked.

Hannah watched the volley. Comments shot back and forth as though both men were in a hurry to conclude the interview.

Medwin waved a hand in the air. "The same he came here with—Enderley, Stoneleigh, Thornton. I think on that occasion the Duke of Harden may have graced us with a visit."

Hannah wondered if that was the source of Lizzie's information about the puppet shows.

Wycliff shut his notebook and tucked it back into his pocket. "I don't think there is anything else to learn here."

"Might I be so bold as to ask to see your puppets?" Hannah asked as the two men rose. Having brought her to a house where supposedly magical marionettes performed risqué plays, her husband should have expected her to want a peek at them.

The half smile ghosted over the baron's face. "Of course. Although they are sleeping, so I ask that you be very quiet."

Sleeping? How odd. Hannah nodded and followed the baron on the balls of her feet as they crept across the floor. The buzz of magic washed over her skin as they approached the large dresser that stood opposite the window.

The baron pulled open a drawer in the middle and Hannah stood close to peer within. The drawer was lined with padded silk in a pale green. Upon it lay two figures, a man and a woman. They wore simple robes of deep blue velvet, as though they had not yet dressed for the day. Each was no taller than twelve inches. Long blonde hair fanned out around the woman's face. Her wooden eyes were closed, but her features and limbs were so expertly carved that Hannah frowned when she could discern no rise and fall of the chest. Her features were exquisite, with high cheekbones and a delicate pink rosebud mouth.

The man had black hair, close cropped to his skull and with a hint of stubble upon his square chin. He had been constructed with broad shoulders and a narrow waist like a storybook hero. All he needed was a sword strapped to his side.

The baron put a finger to his lips when Hannah would have spoken. Then he closed the drawer and led her back to the centre of the room.

The little girl that still resided inside Hannah wanted to grab a beautiful puppet and hug it to her chest, and possibly hide under the table and brush its silken hair. "They are beautiful. Are there more in the other drawers?" She stared at the tall dresser and wanted to pout until he opened all the drawers for her, then had to remind herself that she was no longer a child to be indulged.

"Yes. I have six such marionettes. Another woman and three more men." The blue eye sparkled with humour at her interest while the ruined eye sat like a muddy puddle.

"But they had no strings. How do they move?" Hannah had to ask. Their tiny hands and feet had no wires for the puppet master to control. She assumed this was the magical element of his plays.

"As I am sure you have discerned, they are enchanted and do not require strings. They are rather like actors, and will follow the script they are given. And, like actors, they can be temperamental and don't like to be awakened too early in the day."

They said goodbye to the baron. Hannah wished she could watch a performance conducted by the magical wooden players.

"How risqué are these plays?" Hannah asked as she took her seat in the carriage. They were wooden puppets similar to those used in Punch and Judy shows, and children watched those. Surely they couldn't be so inappropriate as to preclude a married woman's attendance?

Wycliff smiled as he sat opposite her. "Very, from what I am given to understand, and they involve puppet nudity. Perhaps you might ask him to consider something more appropriate for a wider audience, like a Shakespeare play?"

Oh, there was an idea. She might suggest that to the baron, if they had reason to call again. Although why would men want to watch nude puppets? Their clothing was so fine and delicate she wondered if the baron engaged the services of a fine tailor like Daniel Brae to make their outfits.

Wycliff rapped on the roof and the carriage lurched as it moved off. "I have another call to make this afternoon. Do you wish to return home, or visit Lady Elizabeth?"

"Why? I am perfectly capable of being civil, whatever a person's station in life." She had kept a civil tongue in her head, after all, while being mercilessly goaded by Lady Gabriella Ridlington. Hannah couldn't think whom he might question that he considered her an inappropriate companion.

A smile twitched his lips. "While I have some *ladies* to interview, I think it would be best if you were not present. Burroughs frequented a particular establishment to seek out certain entertainments. I need to speak to whichever women he visited."

His words dripped into Hannah's mind one at a time. As he uttered the last one, she gathered them up and discerned his meaning. "Oh." He needed to visit a house of ill repute to question the ladies. Did men find such women tempting, with their wares on open display? She glanced down at her chest. The neckline of her gown was filled in by a fine lawn fichu. "Wycliff?" A small knot of worry spun in her stomach. Their marriage remained one in name only and she was not insensible to a husband's needs. "Have you ever frequented such places?"

"Yes."

Her heart stuttered and she stared at her hands. A lump worked its way up her dry throat and she attempted to swallow it down. Could he be blamed for seeking certain relations elsewhere, when they were not provided within the bonds of matrimony?

Wycliff placed a finger under her chin and lifted her gaze to his. "But not since I married you. While we agreed to a marriage of convenience, I am aware things have...shifted between us. I would never place demands upon you that you are not ready to meet."

Hannah found her voice had quite deserted her. She had only recently discovered that she enjoyed kissing her husband. What lay beyond that seemed rather terrifying, like setting sail on a wide and unknown ocean. She nodded, unable to say anything.

He leaned forward and placed a chaste kiss on her lips. "What would you rather do this afternoon?"

The kiss reminded her of the many things she had to share with her dear friend. "I should like to visit with Lizzie, thank you."

10

Wycliff deposited Hannah in Mayfair to visit with her friend, and promised to return within two hours. From the flare in his wife's eyes, he wondered for one brief, and no doubt ridiculous, moment whether she might have experienced a pang of jealousy at the idea of him questioning the courtesans. Then he gave Old Jim their next address and was met by raised eyebrows and a gruff admission that the man knew his way there.

At his next location, Wycliff stood on the footpath and stared up at the building. La Perfumeria inhabited a smart town house in a row of terraces. Lights in hues of soft yellow, cloudy blue, and pale red bordering on pink shone through the windows and laughter drifted from within. Figures moved behind the gauzy curtains like a shadow puppet show that made him think of the performances put on at Medwin's house.

Wycliff had spoken the truth to Hannah and had not frequented such an establishment since their marriage. Not that he had ever stepped into such a high-end sporting house as this one. Restraining his nocturnal activities was not solely a budgetary consideration. Why waste coin on something he could adequately take in hand himself? The stirring within him demanded loyalty to his wife, even if they lived separate lives.

But that could change. A warmth dwelt in her gaze when he stared into her eyes and when he took her in his arms, she moulded to him and seemed receptive to his kisses. The only problem was his ineptitude at a gentle wooing. Never before had he actively sought a woman's affection. It seemed easier to sneak behind enemy lines armed only with a fork than to determine a way to win his wife's heart.

As much as he was loath to admit it, he needed help of the romantic kind from someone with far more experience. One name leapt to mind. A man who had offered his assistance previously, albeit with a different aspect of Wycliff's life: Sir Ewan Shaw. The man was legendary for his ability to make both men and women fall in love with him. If only Wycliff could set aside his humiliation at seeking help with such a delicate matter. He'd rather reveal his true nature as a hellhound than admit he didn't know how to woo the woman who had slipped so quietly into his mind and heart.

He set aside such thoughts as he approached the bright red front door. Two large men stood on either side of the wide porch and glared at him.

"I need to speak to whomever is in charge." He stopped on the top step as they surveyed him.

"Do you have an appointment?" one asked, his upper lip pulling up in a sneer.

An appointment? He resisted the urge to snort. It was a brothel, not a solicitor's office. "I am Lord Wycliff and I am investigating a death on behalf of the Ministry of Unnaturals. You can either fetch the madam to speak to me in private or I can return with a magistrate, a warrant, and a horde of Runners."

The two men shared a glance and shrugged in unison. One headed inside and Wycliff inspected his fingernails while he waited on the doorstep, like an unwanted creditor.

Five minutes later the hulking guard reappeared and held open the door. "Madam Russo will see you."

Wycliff was led through a lush foyer decorated in dark wood and tones of deep red and gold. Palms in blood-red pots stood against the walls and green foliage reached up to the ceilings. The doorman opened a dimly lit office. Rugs in different tones of deep red and buttery yellow were piled upon each other underfoot. His boots sank into them as he walked. The walls were dark panelling, relieved only by flickering lights in golden sconces.

The madam rose from her desk and gestured to a chaise before the fire. Short and amply proportioned, she might have been a beautiful woman once, but time had waged a battle upon her face with deep lines carved into her brow and around her lips. Her ample décolletage reminded him more of wrinkled tree bark than skin. A too-bright yellow wig sat upon her head and deep yellow silk covered her form.

Wycliff wrinkled his nose. He'd rather stand than sit too close to her. Perfume wafted from her skin and tickled his nostrils, the sweet odour more offensive than the stink of death. At least corpses couldn't help how they smelled. This woman willingly doused herself in whatever concoction created a cloud around her.

"Lord Wycliff, whatever is this matter that brings you here? We have committed no crimes under this roof." She swept her diaphanous skirts out of the way to sit.

Wycliff took up a position by the fireplace a reasonable distance away, then tucked his hands behind his back. "I am here concerning the recent death of Lord Peterson Burroughs. I am tracing his movements prior to an unusual illness that struck him down a month ago. His valet said he much frequented this establishment."

A repetitive thump came from the floor above, accompanied by the occasional feminine gasp and masculine shouted exclamation. How was he supposed to have a serious conversation under such circumstances? Wycliff tensed his jaw until a tic set off in his cheek.

Madam Russo laughed. "Oh, him. I thought you might have had a special request for yourself. I've seen your type many a time—all broody and tortured. Most seek a partner who is wild and uninhibited. Passion is a battle to be fought. Victory grasped only when exhausted and covered in bite and nail marks." When he didn't answer, she continued, "Or are you one of those who need something quite different? A partner who is sweet and submissive, allowing you a chance to be tender and experience the rare inner peace that gentleness brings?"

Wycliff clenched his hands into fists behind his back and buried the outburst that wanted to claw up his throat. Hannah would bring him peace. Tenderness with her would be repaid a thousandfold upon his damaged soul. So long as he could control himself and not terrify her with the dark depths of his impulses. Was that what stopped him from taking her in his arms? A misstep might ruin his chances at happiness forever. Not to mention whatever punishment her powerful mother would inflict upon him.

He mentally swatted those thoughts from his mind. "I didn't come here to discuss my needs, but the appetites of Lord Peterson Burroughs. Did he have a regular woman?"

The madam let out a sigh and gazed up at the ceiling. A loud shout from above was followed by silence. She drew one hand over her bosom and around the edge of her gown. "Penelope. He liked a woman to be prim and proper but with a little bite."

"Bite? So you have a vampyre upon the premises." He drew out his notebook. Any vampyres in England would require strict supervision, so that they didn't deplete the population with their thirst for blood. Perhaps there was another opportunity for Unwin and

Alder. The firm that supplied the *pickled cauliflower* to the Afflicted could investigate a new product. One they could euphemistically call *claret* or a *bordeaux*.

Madam Russo waved a hand. "I assure you, my lord, all my employees are quite *alive*. Besides, it is no crime for a woman to nibble upon a man in the throes of passion."

"It might be when I am investigating the death of a man drained of every drop of blood in his body." At least now he had a name. If Penelope turned out to be both princess and vampyre, it would bring his investigation to a speedy conclusion. "I need to speak to this Penelope."

"I'll see if she is available. More than one lord likes to think he is lifting the skirt of a proper virginal maiden." She levered herself up from the settee and walked to the door.

"Is there anything else unusual about Penelope?" Wycliff asked as he followed.

The madam paused with one hand on the door-knob and raised one eyebrow. "Unusual in what way?"

"Is she any type of Unnatural, or an aftermage?" The woman might not be a vampyre, but there were many other types of creature roaming the countryside.

She cocked her head and a piercing stare stabbed through him. "Neither, as far as I am aware. Do your tastes run that way? We do have a panther shifter who is very popular among certain types. Or there is a young aftermage on my staff who has a fascinating gift —the ability to enhance experiences by adding things not visible to others. It's quite an enthralling skill—he can make you see and experience things that are not real. As though you became an actor in a play only you can perceive."

"For today, I need to talk to Burroughs' regular courtesan. When I have finished, I shall collect a list from you of all the Unnaturals on the premises. They are required to be registered with the Ministry." He had better things to do than fling open doors and discover what lay behind them in an adult version of hide-and-seek.

The woman's eyes widened and then the courtesan dropped over her features. She smiled and took his arm. "Of course, my lord. Whatever satisfies you."

In the foyer, she gestured a young lad over. The boy was no older than ten, and dressed in a red and gold uniform like a footman in a large house. "Freddie, run up and see if Penelope is free. His lordship here wants to talk to her about Lord Burroughs."

"Yes, Madam Russo," the boy said in a formal tone. Then he ruined his impersonation of a proper footman by running up the stairs, taking them two at a time.

Five minutes later the lad ran back down, stopped at the foot of the stairs, and composed himself. He approached with slower steps. "Miss Penelope is indeed free."

"Show Lord Wycliff up." The madam waved toward the upper floor. "I shall compile the list you require," she murmured. Then she took herself, and the cloud of perfume, back to her study.

Wycliff climbed the stairs as the sporting house came to life around him, as though he had arrived at the change of clients. Men spilled from rooms and down the stairs. Some clutched drinks in one hand. Others were still doing up their breeches. Women leaned on door jambs wearing scant pieces of flimsy fabric.

Freddie stopped at an open doorway, rapped on it, and poked his head in. "Lord Wycliff to see you, Miss Penelope."

Wycliff stepped inside and prepared his nose to be assaulted by cheap perfume and stale sex. Instead, he found the air scented with vanilla. Candles burning on the mantel and a low table were the origin of the aroma. The room looked like many other boudoirs. A large four-poster bed stood against one wall. A mirrored dressing table had the stool pushed out as though the owner had only recently risen from it, after fixing her appearance.

A woman sat on a chaise facing the door. Prim and proper Penelope lived up to her reputation. The cool blonde, dressed in a white muslin gown, rose to her feet to curtsey as he entered.

"You wish to speak to me, my lord?" she said in a breathy tone as she gestured for him to be seated opposite her.

"Yes. I understand Lord Peterson Burroughs was a regular of yours?" Wycliff cast around for somewhere to sit and chose a simple wooden chair at an angle to the chaise. He pulled out his notebook and crossed one ankle over his knee to form a writing surface.

Penelope took her seat and folded her hands in her lap. "Yes, my lord. But I have not seen him for some time now."

"That's because he's dead. He died earlier this week and I am investigating the circumstances of his death."

The woman gasped and placed one hand to her chest. The other clutched at the back of the chaise. "Surely you do not think I am involved?"

He stared at her, trying to discern if she were alive or dead. She had the pale colouring of a vampyre and blue veins ran under her delicate skin. "Madam Russo tells me you like to nibble on your clients. Are you a vampyre?"

She closed her eyes and turned her head away. "That is a rather impertinent question, my lord."

"Are you or aren't you?" Impertinent or not, it was a simple yes or no question that required an answer.

She smiled without revealing her teeth. "Of course not. Such things only live on the Continent," she said in a low murmur.

He wasn't convinced, nor would he take her answer as conclusive. The presence or absence of a pulse would settle the issue. He rose to his feet and tucked away his notebook. He had only to place a hand to her throat to know the answer to his question.

At that moment, two young men burst through the door and fell to their knees. "Oh, Princess Penelope, we have come to worship at your feet," they said in unison.

"We're busy," Wycliff bit out at them.

One stood and frowned at Wycliff. "I say! You're not in the book and we've paid for our time here."

The other one climbed to his feet. They both had the flushed faces of men who were sufficiently inebriated as to leave good sense behind.

"I must insist you leave, my lord. These gentlemen have travelled some distance to see me." She gestured to the bucks and smiled upon them.

"Do you or don't you have a pulse?" He stepped forward, one hand outstretched, intent upon feeling for the main artery in her neck.

One of the men cried out and lunged at Wycliff. The fop latched on to his arm and hauled him back. The other called out the door, "Help! He's attacking Penelope."

Soon a crowd gathered in the room, with far more men than he could comfortably take on unless he wished to unleash the hound. He let out a sigh. There was more than one way to get to the truth.

"This matter is not resolved," he said. Then he straightened his cuffs and left.

THE NEXT MORNING, Wycliff called at the imposing Mayfair mansion of the Duke of Harden. The old family name was closely associated with power and wealth. Unsure of his reception, he presented his card and steeled his spine for the expected argument. The quietly efficient butler conferred with his master, and then led Wycliff through to a study without so much as a sniff of reservation about his presence.

"Wycliff, come and have a seat," Harden called. He rose from behind a desk littered with papers and gestured to the armchairs positioned to take advantage of the fireplace.

"Thank you for seeing me," Wycliff murmured as he took a seat.

"You are the husband of my future wife's dearest friend. I imagine we will be much in each other's company over the coming years. But I presume this is no social call?" He smiled, but tired lines pulled at his eyes. Light streaming in through the window emphasised his pale complexion. His normally gold hair seemed dull and appeared tortured, as though it pined for a good brush.

"No, I need to speak to you about Burroughs. I understand he was in your circle." Wycliff settled back in the chair and soaked in the quiet atmosphere that seemed to waft from the many books lining one wall.

Harden let out a sigh and leaned back in his chair. One hand twitched on his knee. "Yes, but we had grown distant in recent years. I've not seen him for some weeks."

"Oh? Some falling out?" Perhaps some dispute between them that had turned murderous? A man with large resources could procure a vampyre as an assassin. Not that Harden looked the type to coldly dispatch his enemies. He seemed more the genial type who carried sweets in his pockets to distribute to children.

Harden waved a hand and then pressed it to the bridge of his nose. "Our fathers were close associates and I think it was expected that we would likewise fall into step. As we grew older, I realised we had differing viewpoints about the world. That circle cares only about being entertained and I...well, I care more in general."

Wycliff filed that odd statement away, wondering what the duke cared about. Then he pressed on. "Can you recollect what you did the last time you were out with him?"

Harden ran a hand through his hair, found a tuft, and then tried to pat it back into place. "Fletches, most probably. Then to Medwin's. The other lads like to visit La Perfumeria and I always part company with them at that point."

"Not to your taste?" Wycliff asked. It was almost expected for someone of Harden's rank to have a mistress set up in an expensive town house.

A smile crossed his face and erased all signs of fatigue. "I am engaged and happen to be madly in love with my fiancée. I know that isn't fashionable among our set, but there it is."

Wycliff stared at the duke. Normally a man in possession of such a title and vast fortune would be selfish, pompous, and a wastrel. Instead, Harden genuinely loved his future wife, retired early of an evening, and appeared to actually do some form of work.

"You're not what I expected." Wycliff knew the duke had a reputation for common sense, but had assumed closer inspection would reveal the vices he kept well hidden.

"I came into my title at a tender age, being only five years old when my father died. I am fortunate in that my mother possessed an intelligent head on her shoulders. She raised me to appreciate how our income was generated. Along with Latin and fencing, I learned business management, farming, and shipping. When I came of age, I took an active role in managing my estates." The duke leaned forward, a keen light in his eyes. "Here's the thing that most chaps fail to grasp, Wycliff—a position of privilege is just that. A privilege. Many families rely on me for their income, and it is beholden upon me to have a care for them. I could not in good conscience gamble away in an evening what would keep one of my tenants in comfort for a year."

Wycliff suppressed the urge to laugh. Before him was a creature as rare as a unicorn—a wealthy landowner who...cared.

11

THE NEXT EVENING, excitement tingled along Hannah's arms as she sat at her dressing table. Attending a dinner party at the duke's home seemed so...grown up. As young girls, she and Lizzie had spent many a night pondering what the future held for them, and now those fanciful dreams were being made real.

Mary fussed with Hannah's hair and, for once, Barnes made himself useful holding the pins. Even more surprisingly, Mary let the disembodied hand assist without screaming, fainting, or swatting at him with the fire poker. The two appeared to finally be on friendly terms.

"There, my lady, all done, and don't you look lovely." Mary placed a jewelled pin in Hannah's upswept dark locks and the small diamonds sparkled. The pin had been a gift from her parents when she had turned twenty-one and resembled a spray of stars.

"Thank you, Mary, and you too, Barnes. You have

been most useful and I am glad to see the two of you managing to get along." Hannah turned to survey the artful curls that brushed her cheeks when she moved.

Mary had outdone herself this evening, and she seemed to be poised and focused of late. Hannah suspected that Frank didn't have a magical effect only on the horses. His calming gift worked on nervous maids, too.

"Well, there's much to do around here and I'll not say no to an extra hand." Mary tidied away the combs and pins on the dressing table.

Hannah bit back a laugh, not sure if the maid's joke was intentional or not. Either way, she embraced the serene atmosphere that settled over the house, now that all the residents had adapted to each other. She picked up a shawl from the end of her bed. The orange silk matched the border around the hem of her gown and was edged with red tassels. Hannah pulled it around her shoulders as she descended the stairs.

Wycliff awaited her in the foyer in his stark evening wear. He flashed her a smile and held out his arm. "You look lovely. Fiery colours suit you."

"Thank you. Your cravat has a fine knot this evening." Hannah leaned closer to admire the tight and well-formed knot.

"Your father tied it for me. Apparently my first effort looked like it had fought a hedge and lost," he admitted as he opened the front door for her.

The carriage pulled them to London and the duke's home in Mayfair. As Hannah emerged into the night air, it carried a sharp nip that made her think of vampyre teeth nibbling at her bare skin. Did one stalk the streets of London, looking for its next victim to drain of their blood?

She tore her mind away from such thoughts, and instead regarded the facade of the imposing house as Wycliff joined her.

"A grand old home, is it not?" He took her hand and tucked it into the crook of his elbow as they walked up the stairs to the front door.

"Yes. I can scarce believe my childhood friend will be mistress here in only a few more days." An ache shot through Hannah at the thought of Lizzie's impending marriage. They were no longer two girls giggling under a blanket, and she would miss the childhood they'd shared. Now, that friendship would change, as they supported each other through the next phase of their lives as married women.

"Welcome to my future home, Lord and Lady Wycliff." Lizzie rushed to greet them, took Hannah's hands, and kissed her cheek. The soon-to-be bride was ravishing in a gown of a deep, dusky pink edged in a soft mossy green, making Hannah think of a rose that had not yet opened to reveal its true beauty.

"Lady Elizabeth. You are looking exceptionally well," Hannah replied in a formal tone as she took in her surroundings.

The floor was laid in black and white tiles, the walls a stark white with marble busts set into recesses. Hannah wondered if one of the ancient busts could be her mother, watching them from behind her veil. The stairs were painted white with a black and white patterned runner to protect the marble. The entrance had a pleasing simplicity about it, although the monochrome palette reminded Hannah of her father's laboratory.

Wycliff stood in the middle of the tiled floor and tucked his hands behind his back, oddly silent for him as he let the two women talk.

Lizzie's blue eyes shone like gems. "That's enough of formalities. You simply must tell me what you think of this old place. It has been over thirty years since anything was changed and of course the late duchess has been gone this year and more. Harden has said that once we are married, I may redecorate however I want!"

"That could be rather a daunting task. I wouldn't even know where to begin." Hannah let her friend lead her to a set of double doors. White was such an imprac-tical colour. It would show every single drop of dirt and blood.

The drawing room had a patterned wallpaper that sought to make up for the austerity in the entrance by being excessively colourful. It mashed together birds and flowers that competed for who was the most garish. If the designer had been content with a single flower or one type of bird, it might have been a more pleasing effect, almost like sitting in a private garden. Unfortu-nately, the designer had chosen dozens of different birds and flowers who all waged war for the viewer's attention.

Hannah met her friend's gaze with laughter burning through her. "This is rather exuberant and...colourful."

"Isn't it ghastly?" Lizzie murmured by her ear. "I intend to have it stripped while we are on our honeymoon. I could not move into this house and stare at the monstrosity every day. It quite brings on a migraine."

Other guests were already present in the drawing room. A finely constructed gentleman conversed with the duke by the fire. Hannah recognised him—he had stalked across her mother's library rugs more than once. Sir Ewan Shaw—lycanthrope.

She glanced at Wycliff, who had stiffened on the threshold. Sir Ewan raised his head and his nostrils flared as he turned to stare at Wycliff. The lycanthrope had the most arresting deep blue eyes and Hannah found herself staring, too.

"Handsome, is he not? Come meet his lucky wife, Lady Alice Shaw." Lizzie steered Hannah toward a slender woman with blonde hair piled up on her head. Serene green eyes, that reminded Hannah of the peaceful glade at her home, regarded the world.

"I believe our husbands are somewhat acquainted," Alice said after introductions were made, a smile twitching the corners of her full lips.

The men in question engaged in a staring contest, though they stood on opposite sides of the room. Wycliff had a tense set to his shoulders and he ground his jaw as though the other man had hurled an insult across the divide. Hannah hoped Wycliff's hackles stayed down and he didn't set fire to his evening jacket. "I do hope Wycliff behaves."

Alice reached out and rested a hand on Hannah's arm. A kind and amused light sparkled in her eyes. "Men who are very similar often find themselves uneasy at being near one another. Let us take comfort in knowing that men of honour know how to behave in polite company."

"Do you think they are alike?" Hannah had not considered that aspect.

In build and colouring there were similarities, but after that they seemed complete opposites. Sir Ewan had a reputation for his impeccable grooming, suave manner, and for being sought after as a guest by many a society hostess. Wycliff hardly cared for his appearance and avoided socialising, snarling like a cornered dog if people ventured too close. Or did lycanthropes and hellhounds share certain other qualities, beyond the obvious changing form and being members of the canine family?

This was the first time Hannah had spoken to the wife of a lycanthrope and she longed to ask a million questions, but to do so would reveal Wycliff's secret.

"Oh, yes," Alice said. "Honourable, protective, fiercely loyal, and with a deeply ingrained sense of justice. We shall have to stay close, Lady Wycliff, in case they decide to start an argument over something. The last thing dear Elizabeth needs is Sir Ewan shedding his clothes and changing form to snap and growl because he got into a bit of a temper."

"Is he prone to doing that?" Lizzie's eyes widened and she fanned herself furiously as her gaze roamed the lithe form of Sir Ewan, finely displayed under his tailored jacket and tight breeches. His cravat looked to have been tied with a mathematical perfection that made even Hannah's handiwork seem shoddy.

Alice laughed and rested a hand on Lizzie's arm. "I am teasing. Rest assured, my husband is usually impeccably behaved."

"But mine is not," Hannah murmured. If her husband kept close to the lycanthrope, would his self-control rub off on the hellhound? Although to be fair, Wycliff's manners at social gatherings had improved much in recent weeks.

Apart from their hosts, Hannah and Wycliff, and the Shaws, there were three other couples in attendance, making an even dozen. The others were drawn from the upper layers of society and known for their respectability. The evening was Lizzie's first foray as a hostess and it pleased Hannah that her friend's fiancé had carefully chosen guests who would be supportive and kind, but entertaining conversationalists.

As Alice excused herself to talk to Lady Glenview, who campaigned with her husband for the betterment of working women's conditions, Lizzie pulled Hannah deeper into the corner by the pianoforte. A tiny frown marred her friend's porcelain brow. "Tell me, Hannah, what do you think of Harden?"

Hannah glanced at the duke, engaged in conversation with the men. "You already know I hold him in high esteem. I cannot fault a man who has such fine taste in a future duchess."

"No, not that. It's that...oh, dear. He has been distant with me of late. I fear I have lost his affection...," Lizzie's voice tapered off to a husky whisper.

"No! Never doubt his love for you." Hannah exclaimed in a whisper so as not to attract attention. "He does appear to be a little tired, but I imagine he has much on his mind. Like you, he is no doubt worried about last-minute wedding arrangements, and he is also planning your grand tour, is he not?"

"Yes, he has taken the entirety of it upon himself and will not tell me a single detail. He wants it all to be a marvellous surprise." The frown remained in place as Lizzie stared at her fiancé, although love burned in her clear gaze.

Hannah squeezed Lizzie's hand. "Everything will be fine. This is only a small bump in the long road you will both share. Only a little more than a week to go and you will see how truly he is devoted to you. When you go on your tour, he will be able to relax and be much restored to his usual self."

A smile graced Lizzie's lips and she kissed Hannah's cheek. "Thank you. I have been quite worrying myself ill that he had changed his mind. You will stay the night before the wedding with me? We can stay up all night and talk, like we used to."

Love for her friend flowed over Hannah and she clasped Lizzie's hands. "Of course I will."

A butler appeared in the doorway and announced dinner. Harden retrieved his future wife and Hannah found Wycliff at her side, offering his arm.

Conversation over dinner was lively and varied. Hannah had Alice to one side and took the opportunity to discuss her aftermage gift. "I understand you can find missing things?"

"Yes, and the opposite—I can hide things if required." For an instant, pain flared in her eyes and then disappeared. "For example, I can alter Ewan's features somewhat, if he needs to conceal his appearance."

"Could you locate a murderer?" How much easier murder investigations would be if magic could lead them to the person responsible. Her mother had tried, but unsuccessfully. Nature placed a limit upon the mages she created, to ensure they could not peek into the minds of others who had no protection against them.

Alice shook her head. "Only if the murderer left a personal possession at the scene. The gift requires me to hold an object that belongs to a person, as I need to establish a connection between one and the other."

"Oh, I understand. If we were ever in such a situation, might we call upon you and prevail upon your gift?" Hannah took a tentative step toward initiating a friendship with the older woman.

"Of course—anything I can do to assist. Your

mother once helped me to find peace. She crafted the bullet that ended Viscount Hoth's reign of terror." Alice's tone dropped low.

Hannah drew a ragged breath. Her mother had told her the tale of the soul eater. He had held courtesans hostage and slowly consumed them until nothing but bones remained. Only two women had ever escaped his clutches. Alice had hidden her soul from him and in a rage, he had abandoned her in Bedlam. Then the demon had turned his ravenous gaze on the famed courtesan Ianthe Wynn, and the Highland Wolves had played their part in rescuing her and ending Hoth. The bullet Seraphina ensorcelled had released a spell within the soul eater and stripped the flesh from his bones as he had done to his victims.

"I am sorry for what you suffered." The words seemed so inadequate to encompass the torture the woman had endured. She couldn't even imagine the level of desperation needed for an aftermage to tear the soul from her body and scatter the pieces.

Alice reached out and squeezed Hannah's hand. "There are many monsters who stalk the parlours of society and hide behind respectability. I do what I can to ensure no woman suffers alone."

"You said our husbands are similar, but I think we are, too. I also strive to give a voice to those who are unable to speak for themselves." Hannah considered how she, too, did what she could for those in a less fortunate position.

"You assist your husband in his investigations?" Curiosity simmered in the older woman's gaze.

"Yes. As I believe you do." Hannah had heard the tales from her mother. Sir Ewan and Alice were like the story of Red Riding Hood and the wolf, as the two worked together to pit themselves against the enemies of England.

Alice sipped her wine and regarded her husband over the crystal. "I cannot sit idly by while Ewan investigates the injustice in the world."

Hannah let out a sigh of satisfaction at conversing with a kindred spirit. "Neither can I. In fact, I believe I rather annoyed Wycliff during our early investigations, when I was adamant he pursued the wrong suspect."

Wycliff's dark gaze met hers across the table at the mention of his name. "I have learned the value of listening to your opinions, Hannah. You also bring a more delicate touch to the proceedings."

Alice winked at Hannah. "A husband who listens to, and values, your opinion is a rare find."

Heat bloomed over Hannah's cheeks at the compliment to Wycliff. With the passing of each day, she came to share that same view—he was indeed a rare find.

THE COMBINATION of good company and excellent wine wrought a magical effect upon Wycliff—he relaxed, and even began to enjoy himself. Stimulating conversation swirled around him on a variety of topics, from politics and support for veterans, to the rights of women. The proximity of the wolf prickled along his hackles and he wondered if Shaw experienced a similar reaction. Although the other man was too damned composed to show it. Wycliff suspected even if his hair were on fire, Shaw would maintain a calm façade.

Lady Elizabeth did an excellent job of ensuring conversation never halted. Her fiancé the duke leaned back in his chair and only coughed politely when the gentlemen became a little too heated. Across the table from Wycliff, Hannah emerged from her shell and sallied forth with her opinions. Quiet satisfaction added to his good mood. His wife proved a match for anyone at the table, and held her own in such company.

He also thought that Lady Wycliff was the loveliest lady present. Not that the other women were unattractive, but they possessed the pale beauty that society praised. Hannah, with her rich chocolate hair and coffee eyes flecked with amber, possessed a dark attraction that tugged at his soul.

After dinner, instead of adjourning to the library or the billiards room, the gentlemen joined the ladies in the drawing room. The women gathered around the pianoforte and Lady Elizabeth selected a piece to play, while another of the ladies sang.

Wycliff took the offered snifter of brandy from a footman and considered how to approach Sir Ewan. He needed to talk to the lycanthrope, as much as proximity made him uncomfortable. The man kept to himself in a corner, staring at a painting, as though he were deliberately setting a trap to lure Wycliff close.

He prowled over and stopped at the other man's side. "There is a matter I would discuss with you, Shaw."

"If it's a recommendation for a tailor, Daniel Brae is a maestro with cloth and needle." Shaw turned from the painting and ran an appraising eye over Wycliff's ensemble.

He stiffened. Part of him whispered that this was his opportunity to seek the advice he desperately needed, but when presented with the chance, he found he couldn't form the words. What if he met with laughter? No, better to stick to business and save the other matter until he was on surer footing with the lycanthrope. "This is regarding my current investigation, to which Brae is loosely connected. He was the tailor for the deceased."

"Ah. So you don't wish to discuss a matter of matrimony, then? Your wife watches us as though she fears we will shed our clothing and go at each other fang and claw," Shaw murmured into his drink. The man wore his good looks with ease and seemed more feline than canine in the way he moved. He lounged with one elbow propped on a bookshelf, as though being in a duke's drawing room bored him.

Wycliff stared across the room at Hannah. She did clutch her glass tightly in her fingers and she kept glancing at him as though judging whether or not to intervene. He flashed her what he hoped was a reassuring smile. He knew when and where to pick his battles. Even with his disregard of civility, he wouldn't start a fight under Harden's roof. Besides, he still embraced a rare good mood that he didn't want to spoil.

He took a sip of his drink to add to the fire running through his veins. "I don't remove my clothes to change forms."

Shaw arched one impeccable black eyebrow. "Really? That would be convenient. I cannot recall how many fine shirts and breeches I have ruined through the need for a hasty shift."

"Nor how many uniforms, I imagine. I heard Wellington made you ride into battle fully clad." Wycliff sought to find common ground with the other man.

Shaw huffed a soft laugh. "Apparently riding naked, while far more convenient, wasn't the *English* thing to do. Even though Sir Manly countered with the fact that we are all Scottish and the Highland Wolves."

"I never saw it, but I hear it was quite the sight." Wycliff had heard the tales of how the Highland Wolves had ridden their well-trained horses straight at the French and leapt from the saddle, changing form in mid-jump to land among the enemy as enormous wolves.

"Are you going to tell me what exactly you are? My wolf smells a certain similarity, but then balks, as though there is a threshold it cannot cross." Piercing blue eyes fixed Wycliff to the spot.

He stared into his glass of brandy and gulped the last of it, finding courage in the mouthful. His wife and her family knew his secret. There were things he hoped to discuss with Shaw that necessitated his sharing that secret. There might also be aspects of living with a shifter that Hannah could discuss with Lady Shaw. "Hellhound."

A black eyebrow shot up. "You spoke the truth about the attack on your men. Many thought you mad, for if the French had such creatures, why did they not deploy them elsewhere?"

Wycliff shrugged. He never questioned why only the company he commanded that day had fallen to the hellhounds, and consigned him to the living hell of being labelled a liar and a coward. "I imagine because they could not be controlled. I would not wish the carnage I endured upon my worse enemies."

He remembered Lady Miles asking who held his leash, and the pull that had drawn him along the inky path to the other realm. But he wasn't ready to confront what sort of master kept such monstrous beasts as servants.

"Were they like you, with a human form?" Keen interest sparked in Shaw's eyes.

"I don't know. I never saw signs of humanity in any of them. Nor did they change at any point while they slaughtered us. The entire time they remained as hell-hounds. But who knows what they did once finished with us." Wycliff wished his glass were full, so he could drown the memories the conversation dredged up.

"Indulge my curiosity for a moment, my lord. How were you created?" Shaw murmured over his brandy.

"A bite, somewhat similar to that which lycanthropes undergo. But this one...burned." Wycliff shot the words out as heat crawled across the old scar.

Shaw stared into his drink and both men fell silent, each lost in thoughts of their transition from fully human to the twilight world where shifters dwelt.

Shaw spoke as the clock over the mantel struck midnight. "Well, as illuminating as this conversation is, you didn't approach me to discuss our similarities and differences. Although I am sure Alice would be delighted to welcome your wife into her sisterhood, if you would allow me to pass this information along?"

Wycliff nodded. "Yes. I think speaking to your wife

may be of comfort to Hannah. She is a woman of many questions."

"With that settled, why don't you ask me what you want to know about vampyres?" Shaw suggested.

Wycliff set his empty glass on the bookcase and tucked his hands behind his back. He thought that the best way to stop himself from doing something stupid with them. "You're the only one who has tracked and killed a vampyre living in England. I need to know if you learned anything about them that will aid in my search for the murderer."

"Despite the fact the French ones are renowned for their appearance and taste in apparel, it is not a universal trait. Forge was ordinary. His very build and colouring, utterly unremarkable. He dressed to blend in. You would sit next to him in a tavern and never take note of his presence." The wolf glanced toward his wife as he spoke. Alice laughed at something Hannah said and the gentle sound added a musical note to the air.

"Did you not sense him?" Wycliff searched for a way to hunt out such creatures. Wolves were able to perform a partial shift, something Wycliff struggled to control, having only done it on a few rare occasions.

Shaw shook his head. "Only when close, his scent abraded my nostrils and set my teeth on edge. But I had to be closer than I wanted for my wolf to recognise the carrion stench that exuded from Forge, and ran the risk that he would tumble to who I was before I had the information I needed. You have an advantage over me.

Does not your other form have an affinity for the deceased?"

"Yes, and the hound perceives the dead differently. But I need to be close and in that form, which doesn't help when I have an entire city to search and appearances to keep up." The hound could take one look at Penelope and see the truth of her nature. But a hellhound hanging around La Perfumeria would cause a panic, given the popularity of the establishment.

"Well, I'd start with Brae if you want some practice," the wolf murmured.

"He's a vampyre?" Instead of contemplating how to scan the thousands of members of the *ton* to find the vampyre among them, the man had just fallen into his lap. Although Hannah had not mentioned his undead status after her visit. Not that Wycliff had asked her to verify whether the man had a pulse or not.

"To the best of the intelligence I have gathered, yes. He lives a quiet existence and I've not heard so much as a whisper of anything untoward about him. He's also the best tailor in England and I personally visit him on a regular basis, so he knows he is being watched." A smile touched Shaw's lush lips. It would be no hardship for the dapper man to be dressed by such a tailor.

"How does he feed?" There were many ways to dispose of a body in London. The tailor could be draining the lower classes and few would notice.

"I believe he has a *larder* that he visits sparingly." Shaw wrinkled his nose in distaste.

Wycliff shared the sentiment. It turned his

stomach to consider how the undead needed to feast upon their fellow men to sustain themselves. At least the Afflicted confined themselves to those already deceased. His attention drifted to Hannah as she moved from the pianoforte to take a seat by the fire. Heat flowed through his veins as he studied her profile. He might find the task horrific, but he would steel himself and pluck brains from skulls for her, if it were required of him one day. "I shall pay Brae a visit. He tried to call upon Burroughs but was turned away, as the man had already taken to his bed by then."

A loud tapping noise interrupted further conversation. Wycliff and Shaw both turned to the window that faced the street. Wings scraped at the glass and long claws rapped on the pane as some creature tried to gain access to the house.

"What on earth is that?" the duke called, as the others turned to stare at the window under attack.

Shaw crossed the room and Wycliff kept pace with him. As they approached, the creature's wings stilled and it gripped the outside ledge. From the feathers and shape of its head, it seemed a large brown owl battled to gain admittance. A flash of cream caught Wycliff's eye. The bird clutched something square in its beak.

With a suspicion crawling into his mind, Wycliff opened the casement. The owl flew inside to a gasp of surprise from everyone else. The large bird would easily reach a man's knees if it settled on the ground. It landed on the back of a chair and gripped the wood with its claws. Then it stretched out its neck to deliver the envelope it carried.

Suspicion confirmed, he thought as he took the offered message. Although he did wonder how all of his new secretary fitted into the owl's smaller frame. "Thank you, Higgs. I see you do work some evenings."

The bird gave him an unblinking stare. Black-tipped feathers encircled its large eyes as though it still wore a pair of spectacles. Apparently, the new secretary did not possess a sense of humour, or perhaps Wycliff had failed in the delivery of his joke. He was new to attempting joviality with people other than Hannah.

The bird rotated its head and then launched from the chair to head back out the window. The duke closed the window before the draft could chill the room.

Hannah joined him. "What is it, Wycliff? And why is an owl delivering messages to you?"

"That was Higgs, the new secretary at the Ministry." He slid his thumbnail under the seal and extracted a sheet of paper. "It would appear my presence is required elsewhere. Lord Stoneleigh the younger has died in circumstances similar to Burroughs. As luck would have it, the consulting physician is Doctor Chartwell, and he reported it directly to Sir Manly, who sent Higgs to find me here."

"Another one?" Hannah turned to Lizzie, torn loyalties written all over her open face.

His wife would want to stay with her friend, but

the call of another murder pulled at her. Given the new information he had learned about Brae, the tailor had moved himself up to prime suspect, assuming loss of blood was to blame once more. Unless there was more than one vampyre moving in society, heaven help them all. "There is no need to ruin the evening for you. I can attend on my own and relay events to you later."

"Nonsense. Of course Hannah must go with you." Lizzie clasped her friend's arm. "She can tell *me* all about it tomorrow."

The duke's staff sprang into action. Cloaks and hats were fetched, and the carriage summoned. In the whirl of activity, Shaw stayed silent and watched with his predatory blue eyes.

Wycliff took Hannah's hand as they left the mansion and he made a silent promise to himself. Now that he had broken the ice with the wolf and revealed his true nature, he would find the courage to ask about a more delicate topic. But first, he had to ascertain whether or not his wife was protecting a vampyre.

13

Hannah clutched her reticule as the carriage lurched forward, and they set off for the home of Earl Stoneleigh, whose eldest son was dead. She considered which of the dozens of questions crammed in her mind to ask first, and decided to start with the most fascinating event of the evening. "Why did Sir Manly engage an owl as secretary? I cannot imagine he would be very good at taking notes or filing, although he is a most excellent courier."

Wycliff sat in the shadows, barely visible dressed in black and with his overcoat concealing his snowy cravat. Secrets further obscured him as he withdrew into his own thoughts. When he spoke, it was in a measured and deliberate tone. "Higgs is what he called a Strigi. He is a man by day and an owl at night. He says the change of light at dusk and dawn triggers his transformation."

"A Strigi? I have never heard of such a creature. I

hope they are not related to the Stryx, which are large birds known to devour babies." Hannah scanned her memory for any mention of mythological birds.

"Why did you not tell me Brae is a vampyre?" Wycliff interrupted her recollection of magical avians. His voice wrapped around her while his form remained partially concealed.

Hannah gasped. The dapper little tailor was a vampyre? Her hands tightened on the reticule in her lap at the thought that she had been alone with an undead creature other than her mother. Then, aware that clinging to the reticule had become a nervous reaction, she set it on the seat beside her and laced her fingers instead. "I cannot impart information I do not possess. When I visited him, I found Mr Brae to be remarkably well dressed and polite. He displayed a pinkish complexion, but it was an artifice from the use of powder upon his skin. I cannot say whether or not he possessed a pulse, as I was unaware I should have been seeking one and both his neck and wrists were concealed by his clothing."

Wycliff extended one hand to his knee and tapped his fingers. He leaned forward and emerged from the literal and figurative darkness he had sought. "Shaw has intelligence that the tailor is such an undead creature and that he keeps a *larder* to satisfy his requirement for blood."

Hannah understood the bristle to her husband's mood. "You thought I concealed such information from you, perhaps to protect him?"

Silence was her answer. Hannah stared out the window to compose herself and didn't turn back until her heartbeat had eased its frantic rush. "If I had suspected him of being one of the undead, I can assure you, husband, I would have mentioned that."

His hand curled on his knee and then straightened out again. "I am sorry. The lack of obvious leads in Burroughs' death preys on my mind. And now we appear to have another such incident to add to the tally. Perhaps the man owed the tailor a sum of money, and instead of a pound of flesh, he sought payment in a pint of blood."

A ghoulish thought, but one that could not be dismissed. "A return visit to Mr Brae will ascertain the truth of his nature and the outstanding debt owed by Lord Burroughs. Mr Brae did mention that a sum was owed. Perhaps we will discover it was a rather large one. It will also present an opportunity to ask if Lord Stoneleigh was a client. I presume young men may all flock to the same tailor if his work is much in demand?" Hannah accepted Wycliff's apology and moved on with the discussion.

"I believe so, but I am not a follower of fashion. *My* tailor also sews clothes for the deceased." A tinge of warmth and humour returned to his words.

Given Wycliff's usual austere clothing choices, she could well imagine a corpse wearing a similar outfit. Colour did on occasion creep into his attire, usually by way of an accent on a waistcoat, but they were rare snatches. Hannah enjoyed those tiny glimpses behind his rigid facade. Since they were discussing clothing, she took the chance to ask a bold question. "The wedding of Lizzie and the duke is not far off. Another visit to Mr Brae would be an ideal opportunity to ask about a waistcoat or cravat to wear that was not intended for a funeral, might it not?"

"Very well. A fitting would be an opportunity for a closer examination of him. Nor would I wish my wife to be ashamed of her husband's appearance at the forthcoming wedding." He had reverted to a measured tone which, she was coming to learn, signalled his reining in a sharper retort.

Hannah reached out and took his hand. "I would never be ashamed of you for such a shallow thing as your choice of clothing. As I am sure you have noticed, I am far from being a devotee of fashion. I merely tried to convey, in a rather clumsy way, that I like the small glimpses into your preferences that are conveyed through a touch of colour or embroidery."

Wycliff kept hold of her hand and brushed his thumb across her palm. "Forgive me, Hannah. It is a long-ingrained habit to take offence, even when none is intended. I still need reminding that you are different from everyone else."

Hannah's heart thrummed in her ears from both the action of his thumb upon her skin and two apologies in as many minutes. "We are both finding our way. I am learning to speak up and be clearer in my meaning."

He nodded and, it appeared somewhat reluctantly, let her hand go.

When they exited the carriage, they found the Stoneleigh household in an uproar. Lights blazed in nearly every window and staff rushed back and forth with no discernible purpose. A high-pitched wail came from the front parlour that assaulted Hannah's eardrums.

"The earl and the doctor await you upstairs," the butler said, when Wycliff stated their errand. Then they were hurried up the stairs to put distance between them and the noise.

Not far along a hall, the butler knocked on a door and opened it upon a state of serenity compared to the chaos that reigned below. An older gentleman, whom Hannah assumed to be the earl, stood immobile at the window. Hands clasped behind his back, he stared out at the night. A younger man sat at the deceased's bedside, his head bowed as though in prayer. Another man of middling years sat at a desk, scribbling upon a sheet of paper.

The man taking notes glanced up at them. "Ah, Lord Wycliff. I am Doctor Chartwell. You may remember me from the untimely demise of Lord Burroughs. I had you summoned as I believe young Lord Stoneleigh's death bears some similarities to that of the other young noble."

"Was it a contagion that claimed them? They were friends and often out together in the evenings." The gentleman at the window turned. Lines pulled at his eyes and the skin of his face drooped as though it, too, had given up on life.

"Earl Stoneleigh, may I present Lord and Lady Wycliff." The physician made quick introductions. "Lord Wycliff, this is Stoneleigh's youngest son, now the new viscount following his brother's sad demise."

The seated man stood to nod first to Hannah and then Wycliff, but he kept his vigil at his brother's bedside.

"Cause of death?" Wycliff stepped closer to the bed.

"My preliminary finding is haemorrhagic shock. You can see that his fingernails and lips have a blue tinge, and he reported dizziness and shortness of breath before he lost consciousness. I also noted his weak pulse and drop in temperature, apart from the other physical signs." The doctor delivered his findings as though he read from an internal report.

"Did you find a puncture wound?" Wycliff asked.

"That is not appropriate to discuss with a lady in the room," the younger Stoneleigh interjected and spread his arm out over his deceased brother, as though to protect him from view.

"My father is Sir Hugh Miles and I am used to assisting him," Hannah murmured as she walked to the side of the bed opposite the younger brother. One look at the deceased and the similarities were obvious. His cheeks were sunken and his skin tone grey, even though he had not been dead for long. The visible skin at his throat and wrists appeared unmarked. To bleed out normally required a severed artery, and a major one at that. She studied the floor under the bed, the blankets, and the pillows, and found everything orderly and clean. Unless the family had cleaned the scene before they, or the doctor, arrived.

The earl turned from the window. "Whether you are used to such disturbing scenes or not, I will not have my son exposed before a woman who is not his mother. Your wife must leave, Wycliff, before the doctor will reveal the location of the wound you seek."

Wycliff drew himself up and Hannah caught his stare. Anger simmered in him at her dismissal, but she would not argue with a bereaved parent. Besides, this gave her an opportunity to ask quiet questions of the staff. She touched his hand. "I shall wait downstairs and leave you gentlemen to your task."

Hannah took her leave of Lord Stoneleigh and slipped through the door. In the hall she approached the hovering butler. "Could you fetch the late Lord Stoneleigh's valet? It would aid Lord Wycliff's investigation to know the locations and people he visited over the last week, and with whom he had been in contact."

"Of course, my lady. Would you care to wait in the study? Her ladyship and her daughters still require their privacy to come to terms with this evening's tragedy." He offered an apologetic look at the fuss still drifting up the stairs.

"Yes, thank you. I would not intrude on the grieving family at this time." Hannah hoped the study had solid walls. While she sympathised with the outpouring, it did make thinking more difficult. Odd how people reacted differently to terrible news. When she'd read of her mother's death, Hannah had fallen numb. Her grief had torn a piece from her heart and stolen her voice, leaving her to cry in silence against Lizzie's shoulder. It had taken days, and her mother's voice issuing from a painting to declare that news of her death was exaggerated, before Hannah could speak again.

The butler showed her through to the study and then excused himself to fetch the valet. Unable to sit still, Hannah walked the room, examining books on the shelves and staring at the sombre portraits. She rubbed the peacock feather ring on her little finger as she walked, to summon her mother.

A serious-looking Tudor-era woman with an enormous ruff around her neck turned her painted head and blinked.

"I am here, Hannah," her mother said through the painting. The lips blurred and reformed as though the artist kept wiping the paint away and trying again to capture the sitter's expression.

"Mother, there has been another death with similarities to that of Lord Burroughs." Hannah craned her neck to talk to the painting. "The life of Earl Stoneleigh's heir has been taken. Could you send Father, please? I assume he will wish to examine the deceased, to confirm whether they suffered the same death. He can also confer with Doctor Chartwell, who is here."

"Of course, dearest. I shall send him on his way immediately. Do you require any other assistance?" The lady rested one hand on the head of a slender greyhound and patted its sleek pelt.

"No, thank you. We shall return home as soon as we conclude here, and I will tell you all." Hannah waved farewell to the portrait.

The picture fell silent as a knock sounded at the door. The butler ushered in a middle-aged gentleman with a worried expression. The corners of his mouth pointed downward and his eyes were heavily lined.

"This is Pike, Lady Wycliff." The butler bowed and exited. The poor man would be run off his feet over the next few days with all the comings and goings in the house.

"Pike, I am assisting Lord Wycliff in his inquiries into his lordship's death. Can you recollect when your master first fell ill?" Hannah perched on the edge of an armchair.

"Would be about two weeks ago, my lady. He came home deep in his cups. I put him to bed, and he slept late and was out of sorts for a day or two. We thought he had caught a cold, what with it still being so damp and chill out. Cook insisted on his drinking a large quantity of bone broth, which seemed to perk him up." The man had a country accent and robust build that seemed out of place in a fine London house.

His tale bore many similarities to that of Lord Burroughs. Neither man had come home declaring a vampyre had waylaid them in the dark and fastened his fangs to a vein. But would a person make such an announcement? Shame, embarrassment, or any number of reactions might have rendered them silent after such an intimate attack. "Did he speak at all of where he went that night?"

The valet scratched his chin and stared at the ceiling. "I believe he enjoyed going to Fletches. Then that baron's house, with the funny puppet shows. After that..." The man's voice trailed off and something at his feet captured his attention.

"La Perfumeria?" Hannah hazarded a guess at what the man didn't want to say aloud.

"Yes, my lady." His jaw tensed and his gaze darted around the room as though he had unwillingly revealed some momentous secret.

"What of the last two weeks? Has he been out and about much, or had many visitors?" Quite apart from being drained, the two unfortunates had also kept to a similar evening routine.

"Not much, my lady. He's not gone out at all the last week, and been in bed well before midnight every night. I'd say the last handful of days, his appearance worsened and no amount of bone broth could put the spark back in his eyes." He twisted his hands together and his shoulders slumped.

There was one more piece of information Hannah needed to elicit. "Do you happen to know the name of his tailor?"

"Mr Brae, my lady. He purchased a new jacket

recently that was delivered last week." Pike's lips were set in a grim line and he appeared on the verge of tears.

"Thank you, Pike, you have been most helpful." Hannah dismissed the valet to grieve in the privacy of his room.

They now had two unusual deaths and both men had not only visited the same establishments in the same order, but both had also been dressed by the same undead tailor.

This time, she would be more prepared for a visit to said tailor. "Better tuck the immobilisation spell into my bodice in case Wycliff causes a set-to," she murmured. Although she wasn't sure which gentleman to use it on.

If a hellhound leapt on a vampyre, who would be in greater need of protection?

14

WYCLIFF CONFERRED with the doctor while they awaited the arrival of Sir Hugh. The earl stood guard, watching their every move as though he expected them to commit some act of defilement upon his son's remains. This young noble had met his end through a wound on his inner thigh, and had been drained via the femoral artery. The location, no doubt, had been why the earl objected to its exposure in front of Hannah.

Once Sir Hugh appeared, the two medical men compared findings while Wycliff conducted brief interviews with the staff. Then he supervised Lord Stoneleigh's being laid upon the floor of the carriage. Sir Hugh sat with the corpse, to ensure he was not dislodged on his journey. Fortunately, Hannah's father had used the buggy to rush to the scene, so Wycliff and Hannah used that conveyance to return to Westbourne Green.

Back at the gothic mansion, Frank moved the body,

taking him in through the tunnel cut underground and that ran from the drive by the house straight to the laboratory level. Hannah fussed with the sheet and rearranged it so all of the deceased remained covered.

"I'll begin the autopsy in the morning. A bit of natural light helps, to make sure I don't miss anything." Sir Hugh pointed to the long, narrow slits in one wall. The mage had installed a combination of mirrors and magic, to direct sunshine from outside through a series of tunnels to release itself into the laboratory.

"Might I have some time alone with the body?" Wycliff asked after Frank had lumbered up the stairs.

Sir Hugh's attention rested on the draped remains. "Mind you don't incinerate the chap, Wycliff. That would make an examination dashed difficult."

"I shall keep my distance. I only want to see if his soul lingers." He met his wife's worried gaze. "I will tell you what I discover."

Still she resisted leaving, until her father tugged on her arm and propelled her toward the door. "Come along, Hannah. Your mother is waiting upstairs."

Once alone with the physical remains of Lord Stoneleigh, Wycliff moved to the far corner and away from any flammable materials and potions. He rested one hand on the stone wall and closed his eyes. Heat flared inside him like striking a flint, and it quickly raced along his veins. Keeping his eyes closed, he lowered his front paws to the cool flagstones underfoot and, drawing a deep breath, he scented death over his tongue. Opening the hound's eyes, he stared at the body.

A dull grey mist filled the room, as though he stared through a light rain. The sheet shimmered ghostly white. But Wycliff alone stood in the room. No souls watched over the remains or sought his attention to point the finger at the murderer. *Blast.* There were a few possibilities as to why he found no trace of the soul. The man could have moved on already, or more likely, his soul might linger in the house where he died.

He leaned against the cool stone walls to let the chill seep into him and dispel the hellhound. Then, knowing he would be unable to sleep, Wycliff returned upstairs to his study. There, he took up a fresh piece of paper and noted all he had learned during the night. Wycliff broke his work for breakfast, to find that room deserted. Barnes scampered along the rug, making a quick exit.

"Barnes," Wycliff called, and the hand froze.

"Where are Hannah and Sir Hugh?" It no longer bothered him to converse with the limb. The thing understood him and responded to his questions, which made it useful, in his estimation.

Barnes pointed downward with the index finger.

"Made a start on the autopsy?"

The answer to that question came in the manner of a thumbs-up signal.

"I shall await their findings, then. Thank you." Wycliff snapped open the newspaper and let the hand continue on about...whatever a hand did to fill in the day.

Later that morning, he returned to his desk and was writing a report for Sir Manly, when a light tread outside his door was followed by a familiar knock.

"Enter," he called out and returned his pen to its holder. "What news of the victim?"

Hannah entered his study with a piece of paper clutched in her hands. A small frown pulled at her brow and he resisted the urge to reach out and smooth it away. "The wounds do not match."

"Don't match?" Wycliff pushed out of his chair and stood. "In what way?"

"They are not an equal distance apart. The punctures on Lord Stoneleigh are one and five-eighths of an inch apart. The holes on Lord Burroughs are one and seven-eighths. Father suggested the angle of entry may have contributed to one's being wider. Or we may have two vampyres." Her fingers crinkled the edges of the paper.

"Two? The last thing we need is a muddle of vampyres taking up residence in the city. We only just manage to allay any fears of the Afflicted. We don't need Londoners learning of another undead creature viewing them as cattle to be farmed and slaughtered." He took the paper from Hannah and stared at the two drawings upon it. In her tidy hand, she had drawn both sets of puncture wounds and noted the exact distance between them.

He pinned up the drawing and leaned one hand

against the wall. "Let us visit Mr Brae and measure his teeth."

She smiled up at him. "I was hoping you would suggest that. I, and my tape measure, will be ready in fifteen minutes."

The tension in his shoulders eased and laughter touched his lips. "Most women would need an hour or more. And before you say it, yes, I know, you are not most women. Let us see who is ready first, you or the carriage."

She was, as it turned out. During the carriage ride, they took the opportunity to discuss the case, not that they had much to share. Mismatched puncture wounds. The absence of a soul. And the fact that Stoneleigh had followed much the same patterns of behaviour as Burroughs: Fletches, Medwin, La Perfumeria—and clothing by Brae.

"The courtesan could be a vampyre. She is known to bite, but before I could feel for a pulse, her patrons dragged me from the room." He recalled her face and the blue veins visible under her skin. Whispers told of a certain erotic pleasure that resulted from the pull of a vampyre sucking the blood from a vein. He could well imagine men with more money than sense paying for such an act.

"You didn't mention that previously. Why on earth did they drag you away?" Hannah's eyes were wide as she stared at him.

He huffed a laugh to ease any concerns she held. "I hadn't paid for her time, and they had."

When they reached their destination, Wycliff helped Hannah down and held the door to the tailor's shop open for her. The interior resembled that of a gentlemen's club, but with rolls of fabric instead of rows of bottles. He inhaled, but did not detect any odour of death—only a tickle of some sweet fragrance that made him want to sneeze. A man stood on a stool and the tailor was in the process of hemming a pair of trousers so they brushed against the polished walking shoes.

"I'll be with you in a moment, Lady Wycliff, my lord," Brae said as he glanced over his shoulder. The tailor plucked a pin from the cushion tied to his wrist and pushed it through the fabric. He sat back on his heels. "You may remove them now, Mr Clarkson, but do be careful of the pins, please."

The tailor rose from the rug and bowed toward Hannah. When his eyes darted sideways to Wycliff, he froze like a rabbit that sensed a hound nearby. Keeping his body immobile, he spoke to Hannah. "Lady Wycliff, to what do I owe this honour? I do hope you are pleased with the lace you purchased?"

"Oh, yes. The lace is quite divine and I have yet to decide how to use it. Lord Wycliff wished to discuss garments for a wedding we will be attending shortly." Hannah gestured to him.

Wycliff glanced toward the panelled door, behind which the tailor's client changed his clothing. No point in loudly asking if the tailor were a vampyre when another was present. He could temper his impatience until the other man left, and afford the tailor a small measure of privacy about his lifestyle.

He met the tailor's clear blue gaze, but stayed silent. Hannah placed a hand on his arm, probably to hold him back in case he shifted form and leapt on the startled-looking man. "The wedding is in only a few days, but with such a lovely range of fabrics, I wonder if you have a ready-made waistcoat that might fit?"

"Of course." Brae regained his composure and walked to the enormous armoire with the doors flung open. A variety of silk, satin, and cotton cravats were stacked in orderly piles. More were strewn with a touch of artistic flair as they dangled from the handles or clung precariously to other pieces of fabric. "Might I enquire what your ladyship will be wearing to the wedding?"

"An orange silk," she replied.

Wycliff recalled the gown—it was the one she'd worn at their own wedding. By a stroke of coincidence, or one nudged into being by the mage, the embroidery around the bottom resembled flames. He thought the deep orange was the most perfect colour on her, if his opinion in such matters counted for anything.

The other man emerged from the dressing room and conducted a brief conversation with the tailor, stared at Wycliff, nodded in Hannah's direction, and then left the shop.

The tailor turned to survey the open wardrobe. "I have some waistcoats that are partially completed, since they are easier to fit. I do believe I have something…"

His voice became muffled as the man thrust his head into the wardrobe to examine the piles of fabrics.

With no other clients in the shop, Wycliff slowed his breathing and half closed his eyes. In quiet moments, outside, he had practiced allowing his vision to shift from one form to another. It didn't always work and early attempts had scorched whatever he stood on, as though the energy shot out through his feet if it could not wrap around his entire form. But lately, it had been more consistent and enabled him to see what the hellhound saw, while still retaining his form as a man.

He concentrated on the heat that lurked within him and drew it upward. In his mind, he imagined lava flowing from his centre, up his neck, and pooling in his eyes. The room shimmered and colours blurred into one another. Next to him, Hannah radiated a soft glow. The tailor, however, was a darker form that denoted dead flesh and the absence of a soul and confirmed that he was indeed a vampyre. Wycliff glanced around the room as movement caught his eye. A gossamer-thin soul fussed with a mannequin in a corner.

Interesting. The vampyre's soul no longer resided in his body, but unlike the Afflicted who remained tethered by a silver thread, this soul appeared free to roam. Did Brae sense its presence? What effect did a removed soul have upon the physical remains?

To change his vision back, Wycliff imagined ice water pouring over him and let the hellhound retreat back to wherever it dwelt.

Brae, unaware of what had happened behind his back, emerged from the wardrobe holding a waistcoat of deep cream with delicate, dark orange embroidery.

"Oh, that is lovely. What do you think, Wycliff?" Hannah turned to him with a smile.

Wycliff fixed upon the tailor. "I am thinking, how can a vampyre live in London without making his presence known to the Ministry of Unnaturals?"

Brae's fingers tightened in the fabric and he gulped. "I don't know what you mean, my lord."

Hannah stepped forward and took the partially completed item from the tailor. "We merely have questions for you, Mr Brae. If you maintain a law-abiding existence, no one is going to haul you off to the Repository of Forgotten Things."

The tailor glanced between them. "I assure you, Lady Wycliff, I do not want any trouble. I simply want to make beautiful clothing from divine fabrics."

Wycliff crossed his arms. Now that he had confirmed the tailor was undead, his hackles reacted to his presence and bristled against the constraints of his jacket as he kept the hound inside him. "Did you feed upon either Lord Burroughs or Lord Stoneleigh?"

The dapper man placed a hand over his heart and his eyes widened. "No! I have patrons who ensure my needs are met on an entirely voluntary basis. I would not harm anyone—especially not a client."

If Wycliff had a guinea for every creature that had told him they meant no harm, he wouldn't be in his current strapped situation. "You didn't extract payment in kind from them?"

The vampyre stared at him, the shorter man's mouth working open and shut. "Most emphatically *not*, my lord. I require my bills to be settled in coin, not blood. One cannot purchase silk with the latter."

That would be easy to ascertain once he saw the tailor's ledgers. "Who are these patrons who meet your needs? I assume they constitute your *larder*?"

Brae turned to Hannah. "Please, my lady, I implore you to respect their privacy."

Hannah patted the man's arm. "Any enquiries we make of them will be discreet, I assure you."

Wycliff bit back a snort. His wife would be the soul of discretion. He had no intention of making assurances he couldn't keep.

Brae's shoulders slumped and he appeared defeated. "I will supply their names, my lady." Then, seeking a more certain footing, he returned to a less distressing subject. "If you wish to try the waistcoat, my lord, I need you to remove your jacket."

Wycliff's fingers curled into his palms for a moment, before he remembered his words to Hannah. He did not wish her to be ashamed of his appearance. The tailor moved around him with caution, making a tuck here and placing a pin there, while Wycliff interrogated him about his origins, how he had come to London, and when he had last raided his larder. There was one subject that particularly intrigued him. "Do you notice your lack of a soul? Are you capable of emotion without it?"

Wycliff searched for any chink to exploit. It rankled to leave the vampyre walking free when they had two unexplained deaths to investigate.

The man's nostrils flared and his gaze hardened. "Unlike some of my kind, I have kept my soul close through being vigilant in embracing my humanity. It takes little effort to retain basic kindness and courtesy."

"Oh, that does sound interesting." Hannah stepped closer. "Is that wisdom passed on to you, or did you come to such an awareness on your own?"

The tailor cocked his head and glanced to the corner of the room where the mannequin stood. "It was like the ebb of a tide. Each day, after I was turned, I lost a little more of myself. I made the decision to actively hold on to who I am and to exercise one act of kindness and courtesy every day."

"A wise and generous decision, sir. If I might be so impertinent, Mr Brae, could I take a measurement of my own?" Hannah asked.

"Of course," he murmured. He fetched a fabric tape measure from the counter, but Hannah pulled her own from her reticule.

She unwound a few inches from one end. "Could you open wide for me? I need to measure the distance between your canines."

The tailor stood immobile. Then he heaved a sigh and opened his mouth. Elongated canines with pointed ends dropped from his upper jaw.

Hannah held up the tape measure. "Two and one-eighth inches. Thank you so much, Mr Brae. I do apologise for the intrusion."

A smile wormed through Wycliff. His wife asked the man to open wide to have his teeth checked, and he complied. If Wycliff had asked, he imagined a tussle would have ensued and he would have had to sit on the tailor's chest and prise open his jaw.

She glanced to Wycliff and he nodded. Brae's fangs were too far apart to have made the wounds on either Burroughs or Stoneleigh.

"Will there be anything else, my lord?" Brae rolled his neck and tugged on the points of his waistcoat. The elongated canines had vanished.

"Yes. A cravat to match the waistcoat." Wycliff grinned and set the man to burrowing into his stash of fabrics once more.

Once they had concluded their business and returned to the carriage, he tapped his fingers on his thigh as he reviewed the interview and the measurement of the man's canines, which didn't fit either victim. "I need to measure the courtesan's teeth to see if they match. How many other vampyres might be living in secret in London?"

"Surely the more pertinent question is how many might have been close to either of the deceased? Mr Brae does not fit the size of the wounds made, nor are they a match for each other. We have gone from no vampyres in London to at least three," Hannah said.

He made a noise in the back of his throat. Once he

returned to the Ministry offices, he would have Higgs enter the tailor in their register. He also needed to ensure those supplying their blood were doing so of their own free will and weren't being coerced. Given that two of the names were female, he would rely on Hannah to ask questions of them.

That made another item tacked to his to-do list. He needed a pay rise to compensate for the amount of unpaid work his wife did as his assistant. Or—another rather controversial idea rattled around in his head—perhaps Sir Manly ought to engage Hannah as an employee of the Ministry.

15

Hannah parted company with Wycliff, as they went their separate ways to talk to the four people who were Mr Brae's patrons. The first woman Hannah visited lived in a charming house in Chelsea. Ivy and roses competed for space as they clung to the stonework of the two-storey cottage. Three young boys played in the front garden, wielding sticks as though they were swords as they fought an imaginary battle. Hannah smiled at them as she walked up the path.

"Who are you?" one challenged, brandishing his stick.

"I am Lady Wycliff and I need a quiet moment with Mrs Harding, if she is available." The door to the house stood open, but Hannah discerned no movement within.

"I'll fetch her." The lad took off at a run, yelling, *"Ma! Ma!"* like a startled lamb in search of the ewe.

Hannah stood on the front porch as a woman

appeared, wiping her hands on an apron. "Can I help you, my lady?" She seemed of a similar age to Hannah, and a dusting of flour lightened her dark hair at one temple where she must have rubbed her brow.

"A private word, if possible, concerning Mr Brae." Hannah stood to one side as the boy flew back out of the house and launched himself at his brothers.

The woman paled and wrung her hands in the apron. "We haven't done anything wrong, have we?"

As far as Hannah knew, there was no law forbidding a person's offering a vein to a vampyre. Although there would be a vocal faction calling for one, if they knew vampyres kept shops on the high street. "No, not at all. I merely wish to ensure that you are his patron on an entirely voluntary basis."

"This way, please." The woman gestured toward an open door and a parlour crammed with wooden toys, laundry, and discarded books. Hannah bent down and picked one up that suffered the indignity of having its front cover bent back over the spine. She closed the book and rubbed a finger along the abused binding before placing it on a table. Patronage, it seemed, paid well enough for the purchase of new books.

Hannah sat on a worn brocade chair and Mrs Harding perched on the one opposite. "I don't mind what he does, and he is very...thoughtful. He only ever calls once a month. No more, he says, so as not to overtax us."

With four patrons, that would allow a visit to one each week on a monthly rotation. Was that sufficient to keep hunger at bay? Another thought swirled through her mind. Why didn't vampyres rot like the Afflicted? It hardly seemed fair.

"How did you become acquainted with Mr Brae?" Curiosity nibbled at Hannah. How did one step into a vampyre's larder? He could hardly advertise in the newspaper.

"Mr Harding delivers Mr Brae's fabrics from the wharves. He came here one day and saw the boys and we got to chatting. It's not easy raising three lads and keeping them clothed and fed. Good Lord, but they can eat." She flashed Hannah a smile and a ruckus drifted from outside through the open window.

"I can imagine," Hannah murmured. "Did Mr Brae raise the issue?"

Mrs Harding frowned and rubbed her temple, which removed the previously deposited flour. "I can't recollect now. He said he would always ensure Mr Harding was well paid if, once a month, I let him hold my hand. It seems harmless enough and the extra coin means the world to my family."

"Does it hurt?" Hannah edged forward in her eagerness to learn how such undead creatures fed.

"No. Only a sharp prick at first, as though I'd caught myself on a pin while sewing. After that, well, it's rather...nice." Her voice dropped to a conspiratorial whisper and a blush worked up her neck.

"I assume he...pricks...your wrist?" Hannah gestured to hers. Since Mr Brae had asked to hold the woman's hand, feeding from the vein in the wrist seemed most likely.

"Yes. He always makes sure I have a cup of sugared tea and a biscuit before he leaves." She extended her right arm with the wrist exposed.

Hannah peered at the skin but not a single scar or blemish marked her wrist. It seemed the tailor did indeed take good care of his patrons. "Thank you, Mrs Harding, you have been most helpful."

"You'll not tell anyone, will you, my lady?" the worried mother asked as she escorted Hannah to the door.

"Of course not. Everything you have told me has been in the strictest confidence," Hannah reassured her, before taking her leave.

Next she paid a call on the other woman, who told a similar tale of a solicitous Mr Brae. He visited once a month and always set tea and a biscuit by her chair before he left. She wondered if Wycliff would find the same sequence of events among the male patrons.

THAT AFTERNOON, Hannah leaned against the wall in her favourite library pose, her legs drawn up under her skirts and a journal in her hand. A pencil hung limply from her fingers as she stared out the window at birds flitting among the trees. Ideas nibbled at the edge of her consciousness as she glanced to the east. Somewhere in London lurked a vampyre other than Mr

Brae, preying on noble young men. But how to unmask the fiend?

There was still the possibility that Mr Brae found his ration of once a week insufficient and drank from his clients. But why drain two men to death, when he laid out tea and biscuits for his female patrons? The actions were so inconsistent. Unless the absence of his soul dictated whether he treated the patron humanely or not. She noted that down as another avenue to pursue.

Wycliff took another approach and searched for a commonality between the deceased men. Hannah studied ways in which a body could be drained through two puncture wounds. She struck through *leeches* on her list. They were far too messy and slow. Her husband's focus on locating the vampyre responsible conflicted with her father's teachings ingrained in her over many years. They did not have conclusive proof that a vampyre had committed the crimes, although she did acknowledge it seemed the most likely scenario.

Could there be such a thing as a leech shifter? Until recently, she had never heard of a Strigi. There could be some other type of immortal creature that dined on the blood of men. A single word bounced around in her mind. *Immortal.* That made her think of another man who stood in place while time flowed around him. Doctor Peter Husom. The young man who had been her father's teacher.

Needing a distraction from a case with frustratingly few clues, she turned to a clean page in the journal and wrote *Doctor Peter Husom* at the top. Memories surfaced of the day in Newgate Prison when her father had confessed that the doctor had not aged with the passage of thirty years. Her father said that the doctor had once confided that the answer was in his name, if anyone looked closely enough.

"It's in his name," she murmured.

Idly, as a form of doodling, Hannah rearranged the letters of the name. Short anagrams formed: *sheep, home, resume, peruse, mothers...*

Her mind took flight with the birds outside the window. Did Immortals cling to such titles as doctor, or would their true name reflect humbler origins? On a whim, she crossed out *doctor*. That left her *Peter Husom* and with a will of its own, her pencil rearranged those letters into...

P-R-O-M-E-T-H-E-U-S.

She dropped pencil and journal and leapt to her feet as though the very word had burned her. The answer stared back at her. The man who had enraged the gods by stealing fire and giving it to humanity. In return, Zeus had sentenced Prometheus to eternal torment. Chained to a rock, every day an eagle pecked out and ate his liver. The organ would grow back overnight to resurrect him by morning. His immortal suffering had only ended when he was freed by Hercules.

His liver.

Ideas collided in her mind and Hannah placed her hands over her ears to contain them. There was only one way to kill a vampyre—remove the liver, the organ of regeneration. One frightening idea dominated her thoughts. Peter Husom, the man who had instructed her father in the medical sciences, was the original vampyre.

Then a voice whispered from the recesses of her mind: *Or was he?* Hypothesize, then strategize, her father taught her. She had a theory—now she needed to determine the truth of it. She also needed to tell Wycliff that the man they had once suspected of using galvanism to reanimate corpses might be draining nobles of their blood.

Snatching up the journal, Hannah hurried out of the library and along the hall. She rapped on Wycliff's study door, only to be greeted by silence. A pull on her skirt caught her attention. Barnes sat at her feet and tugged on the fabric.

Hannah scooped up the hand and raised him to eye level. "Has he not returned yet?"

Barnes waved two fingers sideways in the negative.

Bother. She thought he might have finished his business in London by now, but something must have detained him. "I don't suppose you know when he will return?"

Barnes raised and lowered a knuckle in his version of a shrug.

She tapped her foot and considered her options. She could either wait until her husband returned from London and possibly delay finding out crucial information about vampyres for another day, or go alone.

"I shall go alone. But I will tell Mother of my intentions." It seemed the height of foolishness to confront the person who might possibly be the vampyre who had slain Lords Burroughs and Stoneleigh, and not tell anyone of her whereabouts or take precautions. Hannah set Barnes down on the floor and climbed the stairs to her mother's turret. This knock was answered by leave to enter.

"I believe Dr Husom is Prometheus," she blurted out before she had shut the door. She simply had to tell *someone* of her discovery. "His name, Peter Husom, is an anagram."

Seraphina waved her hands and a purple blob on the workbench disintegrated and drifted out the window as a faint mist. "How intriguing," she murmured.

"The purple mist or my discovery?" Hannah wasn't sure which her mother referenced.

"Both." She wheeled her bathchair around. "I admit to idle curiosity as to the doctor's exact nature, but never had the time to fully investigate. Besides, it seemed rude to poke about in his private business when Hugh holds him in such high regard. If he were Prometheus, that would explain his fascination for scientific investigation."

Hannah crouched before her mother and took her hands. "Mother, you are missing the point. He could be the original vampyre."

"You think he might be your murderer? I find that hard to reconcile with what we know of him. He strives

166

to save mankind, not end it, and works tirelessly at the Chelsea Hospital." Seraphina pulled a hand free to stroke Hannah's hair. Then she returned to her workbench and ran a finger along a neat row of small, coloured glass vials.

Ideas collided in Hannah's mind and tangled together like yarn the puppy had found. "I would find it difficult to believe him capable of murder. But he may know something about their habits, such as signs of starvation, which could aid Wycliff's investigation."

Seraphina selected a vial of deep red glass, where the contents swirled around inside, and pressed it into Hannah's hand.

She stared at the small bottle. "What is this?"

"A mist form of my immobilisation spell, for when you don't want to get too close to someone. Don't open it unless you need it, and make sure the mouth of the vial is pointed toward him. I assume you are going to visit the doctor alone, since Wycliff has not returned from London." Seraphina reached out and closed the hinged lid on a large bottle, where another purple blob crept over the edge. A drop hit her worktable and dissolved in a puff.

"Yes. Would it be presumptuous to ask you to craft him a ring of mage silver? If he had one, you could make him aware of my plans." Imagine if there were a way to speak to each other across distances without the need to rely on letters, giant owls, or her mother acting as relay.

"Already underway, dear child, and nearly ready

for casting." Seraphina waved to a black pot about the size of a closed fist that sat over a blue and silver flame. Slick black fingers pointed up from the brew and then bubbled back into the liquid. "He has to ask, though. He might not want his mother-in-law to be able to find him at any time."

As Hannah trod the spiral stairs down from the turret, she argued with herself over the advisability of her actions. She had called on Doctor Husom before, and found him an intelligent conversationalist. His work with electricity fascinated her. But this time she would ask him to reveal the secret of his origins. What if he became angered?

By the time she reached the back door, she had settled on trusting her instincts. Nothing in her interactions with the doctor had triggered any warning inside her. Besides, if he turned into a monstrous creature, she had her mother's potion slipped into her pocket, where it would be easy to reach.

Hannah found Frank outside and asked him to harness the horse to the carriage. Then she sought out Old Jim inside the stables to ask him to take the reins. She didn't wish to distress the sensitive giant by returning to the Chelsea Hospital, where some of his limbs may have originated.

On the journey to Chelsea, she reassured herself that even if the doctor were some half-starved vampyre, he wouldn't lunge at her in the hospital. There were simply too many people strolling the grounds and corridors. Once at her destination, Hannah trotted through the halls, nodding to the scarlet-clad old men. Her questions as to the whereabouts of Doctor Husom were met with shaken heads.

"Not here today, my lady," one said.

She smiled and thanked him for his time, while inside she plotted her next move. With little idea as to how an Immortal would while away the time, she set off for his Chelsea home. The laboratory tucked up under the roof seemed the most likely place to try.

Her rap on the door went unanswered, so she knocked again, and much louder. Silence echoed beyond the door.

"Bother," she muttered and resisted the urge to kick the cast-iron boot scraper.

Remembering her previous visit, when he had taken several slow minutes to answer the door, she retreated to a seat across the road.

As much as she peered at the windows, she couldn't discern any movement. If she had brought Barnes, could he have scampered up the drainpipes and told her if the doctor laboured in his attic laboratory? Or she might have been able to squeeze the hand through the letter slot? While she pondered ways to use Barnes to facilitate breaking into a house, the front door swung open.

Doctor Husom stuck his head out and glanced around.

"Doctor Husom!" Hannah rose from the seat and hurried across the road before he slammed the door shut.

He stared at her, pushed his spectacles up his nose, and frowned. "Miss Miles. Did we have an appointment I have missed, or do you carry a message from your father?"

She caught her breath on the top step and smoothed the fabric of her dress. "I am Lady Wycliff now, Doctor Husom, and no. We did not have an appointment, nor am I sent by my father. I have another matter I wish to discuss with you."

The frown deepened. "I am rather busy, *Lady Wycliff*. Perhaps you could visit another day?"

"But I am here now, *Prometheus*." She watched his eyes widen behind the spectacles. "There is a vampyre loose upon London and I require your particular assistance."

He heaved a sigh and looked up and down the street. Satisfied that no one had overheard, he gestured for her to enter. "I suppose this conversation is more suited for inside."

Stepping over the threshold, she allowed herself one moment of vanity that she had discovered his secret, hidden in plain sight. Then, as the door slammed shut, she wondered if she should have waited for Wycliff to accompany her. All her rational arguments as to why the doctor had never given any indication of being dangerous seemed to have fled out the door.

Doctor Husom led her through to a sparsely furnished parlour. A plain settee in tones of brown sat opposite a simple leather armchair. The floor had no rug, no ornamentation adorned the mantel, and the walls were bereft of art.

Hannah sat upon the settee and waited for him to take the armchair. She folded her hands over her reticule and considered where to start. "My father is proud that you were his teacher when he was a young man. While he does not know your method of staving off the effects of time, he said that you once mentioned your identity was hidden in plain sight for those who cared to look."

Elbows on the arms of the chair, he tented his fingers. "I prefer the letters of my name arranged as Peter Husom, if you don't mind. The other is a relic from an era no longer remembered by mankind. Let it crumble and return to dust."

She regarded his calm demeanour. So far the revelation appeared to be evenly met. "Am I correct in my hypothesis that vampyres originated with you? They can only be killed by the removal of their liver—the organ of regeneration."

He let out a sigh and one hand moved to pinch the bridge of his nose. "Yes. If one is chained to a rock, with a giant eagle pecking out one's liver every day for years, people eventually start to talk."

16

Doctor Husom turned his face into his palm as he spoke, as though hiding from the memory. "I don't know for how many centuries I endured; time had no meaning for me. Who knows for how long men hid in the trees and watched as the eagle feasted each day? Or why that particular day, they waited until the eagle appeared and attacked it, throwing its corpse into the ocean? I thought they would rescue me, but how wrong I was. They turned their knives upon me."

Hannah gasped and gripped the arm of the settee. A horrifying certainty arose in her mind as to what happened next, but she voiced the question anyway. "Did they remove your liver?"

The doctor took off his spectacles and polished them on the tail of his shirt that had worked loose from his breeches. "Yes. They sliced me open and ripped out my liver. Then they fought over it. They tore off hunks with their bare hands and shovelled the bits into their open maws. Blood covered them as they feasted on my organ and then they turned their crazed eyes to me. One shouted that it wasn't enough, since they all had to share. The last thing I remember is him leaping on me, and pressing his entire face into the wound to guzzle my blood. By the next morning, I was reborn. Blood covered the rock and surrounding grass. Not long after, Hercules released me and I disappeared into the mists of time."

What a terrible way to father a race. One question bothered her. "Why are vampyres undead, though, since the men who fell upon you were alive?"

The doctor spread his hands. "It is possible that feasting on my body made them sicken and die, but the portion of my liver allowed them to regenerate. Although it is my belief that the gods struck them down for their abhorrent behaviour. Our divine masters can be capricious, and punishments they mete out are not always commensurate with the slight committed."

Hannah gathered her thoughts, which had scattered in numerous directions. It seemed so unfair. The first vampyres committed a heinous crime and yet no rot touched their forms. The Afflicted were struck down by a mage using dark arts, and those innocents fought a constant battle against the natural process of death. "I can only assume the regenerative powers of your liver they consumed has kept them and their kin from decaying."

He rested both arms on the chair, more relaxed now that he had revealed his secret. "We will find a cure for the Afflicted, Lady Wycliff, even if our masters will not intervene."

She managed a weak smile. "I hope so. It just seems so..."

"Unfair? Yes. In my observations over the millennia, there is nothing so evil as what one man can do to another. We must take comfort in knowing that the wicked Mage Dupré will have to account for his actions in the underworld."

Or if one knew a hellhound who could journey there, they could find that evil soul and drag its secrets from it. But that wasn't the particular problem Hannah had come to discuss with the doctor. "Did you have any contact with the first vampyres after that?"

"At times. Since they ingested part of me, I could feel when those first few children passed close to me. Over the millennia that sense dimmed, and now, I could stand right in front of one and never know it was a distant offspring."

Which meant no hope of sending him into London to sniff out any others for them. "I have to ask, Doctor Husom—do you require sustenance?"

He stared up at the ceiling as he considered her question. "I have a fondness for Cornish pasties, I enjoy a fine brandy, and I have a particular weakness for a strong cheese. But I do not sup on blood as they do. I believe it is because that was their genesis, not mine. I really don't see how I can help you, Lady Wycliff."

Neither did Hannah. She wasn't sure what she had expected. Perhaps for him to have kept a record of every vampyre that had descended from his body. Or a way to find them among a crowd, rather like using a bloodhound. "I was hoping for any information about their condition you could share that might help us in tracking down the responsible party. I do have one last question, if I may be so impertinent."

"What is it?" He rose from his chair to indicate the interview was at an end.

Hannah stood and followed him from the parlour. "How do you endure it? To have lived for millennia?"

"Why, I continue to learn, Lady Wycliff. Humans are marvellous creatures, ever reaching for more. Only recently, they discovered electricity. Now, how may that be applied? I become excited to contemplate what discoveries await us in the future. I have seen the rise of civilisations and the most incredible inventions, yet I think humankind is not done yet. Imagine if one day they discover how to fly. I quite want to see that." He smiled at her and opened the front door.

Hannah turned his words over in her mind as she walked along the road to where Old Jim waited with the carriage. Prometheus endured by continuing to learn. Fire had not been the only thing he had brought to mankind. Study and the pursuit of knowledge had kept him engaged in a constantly changing world. Her mind spun to consider how his world had altered and evolved to the one she lived in now. What would the world look like in another two hundred years?

LATE THAT AFTERNOON, Wycliff returned from a useless foray to London. His questions went nowhere and he was no closer to finding the killer. As he handed the mare's reins to Frank and asked where to find Hannah, Frank gestured to the forest. Mary merely stared at him with wide eyes. The last hour or so of sun for the day had managed to become pleasantly warm, and he left his riding jacket tossed over the stair railing. Then he stalked through the forest, pushing foliage out of his face. The trees thinned at the edge of the round glade beside the stream. Instead of bursting upon the scene, he leaned upon a gnarled trunk and took a quiet moment to contemplate the peaceful tableau.

Hannah lay on a tartan blanket with cushions piled under her head. She held a book and was reading. The sun caressed her hair and highlighted caramel tones among those of deep chocolate. The water burbled as it flowed over rocks. Percy the peacock sunned himself, and his harem of peahens sat in the shade under arching shrubs.

Once, Wycliff had thought he had nothing to live for. Now, he had found something worth holding on to. He also contemplated how a marriage of convenience could turn into something rather inconvenient. A warm intimacy had sprung up between him and Hannah and he loathed the thought of trampling over it and losing her affection. He wanted more, but proceeded with caution. If she glimpsed how hunger gnawed at him, she might take fright and have her mother turn him into a carp.

Another thing held him back. He still clung to his secrets and he did not want them to fester and spoil what grew between them. Making a decision, he stepped out of the shadows and crossed the lush lawn to his wife.

"May I join you?" he asked as he approached.

Hannah dropped the book to rest open, face down, on her chest. "Of course."

He stretched out beside her, positioning a blue-and-yellow-checked cushion under his head. Hannah remained silent and did not fill the void between them with conversation. A trait he admired in her. He let the companionable silence seep into his weary bones. Secrets became heavier the longer you carried them, and he longed to let go of his burden.

Without preamble, he set his story free. "It was the autumn of 1814, and while we didn't know it then, we neared the end of the Peninsular Campaign. I was sent out with a platoon of men on a reconnaissance mission, and we were returning to the main regiment."

Beside him, Hannah closed the book and placed it on the blanket at her side. She laced her hands over her stomach and waited.

"We made camp for the night at the edge of a forest, a few miles from a small village. As the officer in charge, I arranged the men into shifts to guard our slumber. Then I used my saddle as a pillow and curled up in a blanket to snatch a few hours' sleep."

He swallowed as memory flashed through his mind.

Images burned into his brain that would never be expunged.

"The screams awoke me. The high-pitched cry of horses in pain and blind panic. They tore free of their tethers and bolted. The men I set as sentries fired upon whatever had spooked the horses. I grabbed my rifle and sword as chaos erupted around me. Three of them emerged from the shadows. Nearly the same height as a man, with eyes that glowed red in the dark. Heat rippled around them and when we fired, our shot melted before it struck and lumps of metal fell to the ground."

"How many men were with you?" she asked in a soft tone.

"Thirty. The hellhounds tore them apart as though they were made of bread. Pieces flung about. The air stank with the sharp odour of excrement, blood, and charred flesh. I fought. We all did. But nothing made any difference. Anyone who got close enough to use a sword suffered burns, and I didn't see a single blow land. I held up my arm in front of my face to fight, but couldn't see what I struck at. Then, I admit, I simply gave up. One beast stalked toward me and I dropped my sword. I knew I was defeated and it would rend me limb from limb. I fell to my knees and bowed my head, waiting for death. In those moments, my only thought was how no one would mourn me. There was no one to notice my passing, and the estate would go to some distant second cousin I have never met."

Hannah rolled to her side and placed a hand on his chest.

Wycliff rested his hand over hers. "Around me, the screams continued. Some men cried for me to help, to do something. Others shouted that I was a coward, as they died with useless weapons in their hands. The hellhound sat before me. It did nothing except watch. My skin prickled with the heat rolling from it and my throat scorched. When silence fell and all my men were dead, the other two joined it. I thought that perhaps as captain, I was to be their final meal. Like the coward I was, I hoped they made it quick. The stench of burned bodies filled my nostrils and choked down my throat. I couldn't see that a far worse hell awaited me."

"What happened?" Hannah whispered.

"I pulled at the collar of my uniform and arched my neck. I thought a strike to the jugular would bring a fast end, so that I might not feel it when they tore me apart. The largest one of the three approached until my clothing smoked from its presence. It opened its jaws and bit me where I had exposed my throat. I confess the pain was excruciating as white-hot fangs dug into my flesh. Its saliva was liquid fire. As I screamed and prayed for death, I lost consciousness." Wycliff closed his eyes and the old scar at his throat burned anew.

Hannah nestled closer to him and Wycliff put his arm around her. For a long time, the two of them lay in near silence. Only the gurgle of water and the soft conversation of the peahens drifted over them. Moment by moment, the old pain ebbed.

"I awoke to the tug of someone pulling off my boots. Women from a local village, searching the chunks of my men for anything worth selling. I waved the girl away and probably scared her half to death. My neck burned and pain made black spots dance before my eyes. Somehow, I made it to my feet and, finding no one else alive, I wandered for three days until another patrol found me." He had lost count of how many times he faded in and out of reality, waking to find himself face down in the dirt. A plaster of mud brought a small amount of relief to the wound in his neck. He recalled his surprise on finding the flesh and his left arm still intact, given his memory of the hellhound ripping out chunks of his flesh.

Hannah sat up. "Did you tell them of the hellhounds?"

"Yes. None believed me except Sir Manly, who created the Highland Wolves. Even then, we found no trace of the hounds. They attacked my men and then vanished back into the night, never to be seen again. I was labelled a coward for surviving when my men did not, and a failure as an officer for losing the entire platoon. Some even said I was a traitor and must have purposely led my men into an ambush." Some among his superiors demanded he be shot for his failures. Wycliff had spent days in shackles while his superiors argued over what to do with him. Eventually, they sent him back to England in disgrace.

Worry pulled at her eyes. "Did you not show them the bite? Surely that evidence would convince others of the truth of your words?"

Wycliff closed his eyes and drew a deep breath through his nose. He had started down this road and there was no turning back. Instinct told him that of anyone in the world, Hannah would understand. "I never showed anyone. To do so would expose my greatest shame—that I had surrendered. I had tossed my weapon to the ground, crouched in the dirt, and waited for them to end me."

Hannah leaned over him. Tears shimmered in her eyes and one rolled down her cheek.

He caught it on his thumb. A perfect, luminescent globe more valuable than any jewel. "You would weep for me?"

"Yes! For all you suffered and endured in silence, with no one to believe you or be at your side as you healed. Because you *would* be mourned. My life would be infinitely colder without you in it."

He moved his hand to her nape and pulled her to him, claiming her lips in a slow kiss. She sighed against him and pressed closer. Holding her near, Wycliff rolled and settled over her without breaking contact with her lips. Then, he captured one hand and held it by her head as he rained kisses on her jaw and down her neck.

Never in all his pain-fuelled nightmares could he have imagined his survival would be rewarded with such a treasure. Then, before he forgot himself and sought too much, and knowing his wife would have ideas swirling in her mind, he let her go.

"I imagine you have questions," he murmured.

"Yes. Several." Her eyes shone with an entirely different emotion as she sat up and folded her legs under her. A slight tremor shook her hands as she smoothed loose strands of hair off her face and tucked them back into place. "You said that the bullets you fired melted, and that anyone who stood near enough to use a sword suffered burns. Yet the day at the Pennicotts' when your hackles appeared, and again when you changed form here, I was able to stroke your fur. I did not find you hot at all. I would have called you pleasantly warm. Why was I not burned?"

Once she had composed herself and lowered her hands, he took hold of one and laced their fingers together. A selfish move, but he craved the continued contact. "I have been thinking about that and believe there are a few possible reasons. One is because I swore to protect you and would never harm you."

"Hellhounds are protectors of the dead. I wonder if part of you can sense the curse frozen within me? And obviously my mother is deceased." A line creased her brow as she glanced up at a sparrow flitting overhead.

He narrowed his gaze at the small bird that lingered on a nearby branch. Was the mage spying on them? "Possibly. Your mother once advised me to find an anchor or a safe harbour. I think she meant a way to maintain my humanity, so I did not become lost in the creature's hell. I believe you are that to me—a reminder of all that can be good about the world."

Hannah rested her other hand over their joined ones. She glanced up at him before lowering her gaze to stare at the abandoned book. "I am glad that our marriage contains unexpected benefits for both of us."

He tightened his grip on her hand for a moment. Should he say something about other marital benefits they could both enjoy? Then the moment passed, as Percy let out an ear-piercing cry and flung up his tail feathers in a display for his peahens.

Another question lit her eyes with amber fire. "Can you control the heat you radiate? Perhaps it is a protective measure to negate weapons used against you?"

That was another, as yet untested, theory. "I have some control over the intensity of the heat I emit. When anger flows through me, I burn hotter."

A glint of mischief crept into her gaze. "If you could generate enough heat to melt a bullet, think how quickly you could heat bath water."

Wycliff stared at her. Yet again she chose to look for the positive in a situation. He raised their joined hands and kissed her knuckles. "Perhaps we should return to our investigation? If Daniel Brae is not our vampyre, we still need to continue our search."

"Ah! I have some intelligence to share on that topic." Hannah let go of his hand to pick up the book.

Wycliff climbed to his feet and held out a hand to help her up. "Oh? What have you learned?"

"What do you know of Prometheus?" She gathered up the blanket and cushions.

"As much as I learned at school. Is his fate relevant to this investigation?" Wycliff opened the hollowed-out tree trunk to put away the blankets. Then he dropped the lid and took hold of her hand again as they returned through the trees.

Hannah held up a hand to push away foliage that grew over the path. "I thought the father of all vampyres might have some insight into how to track down our murderer. But unfortunately, he has little to do with his offspring."

He stared at her. While he had been out questioning the tailor's *larder* and following the movements of the victims, his wife had found Prometheus. "I think a drink may be called for, while we exchange tales."

HANNAH SPENT an enjoyable evening with Wycliff, as they caught each other up on what they had learned. She even received a kiss on the lips when he said good night on the stairs and every part of her, down to her toes, vibrated with happiness.

The next day, as she sat on the sofa in the library, a loud squawk followed by a thud interrupted her reading and made her eyes roll.

"Barnes," she muttered under her breath.

A tap on the toe of her shoe made her glance down. Barnes sat on the carpet and waved the index finger back and forth in what Hannah took as an *it wasn't me* gesture.

Hannah frowned. "Well, that is strange. Let us investigate."

The limb trotted alongside Hannah as she entered the front parlour to find an odd sight. Wycliff stood by the fire, his arms crossed and the fingers of one hand pinching the bridge of his nose as though something pained him. Frank knelt on the floor with the slumped Mary cradled to his chest. The patchwork man growled up at Wycliff.

Hannah stopped once over the threshold. "What is going on? Did something frighten Mary again?"

Frank growled and pointed to Wycliff. Hannah took a step toward her husband and swallowed. There was one way in which the fragile Mary might be terrified of Wycliff and faint dead away. Had she seen the hellhound?

Wycliff released the bridge of his nose and lowered his arm to the mantel, where his nails rapped on the wood. "I merely asked if she was up to performing a task for me and...this...happened." He swept his free hand toward Frank, who stood with Mary in his arms.

"You made a request that caused her to faint?" Hannah thought Mary had made great improvements with her nerves as Frank's calm demeanour worked on her. How sad if she had a relapse of skittishness. Hannah was too fond of the young woman to sack her.

"It was a somewhat...unusual request." Wycliff glared at the woman's prone form as she uttered a faint moan and began to rouse.

"You may as well tell me what it was, before my imagination begins suggesting horrendous things a lord might ask of a maid that results in her fainting." Hannah swallowed her doubt there would be a simple answer here.

Wycliff's nails rapped a few more times. "It

concerns the investigation. There is a small group of women who are not forthcoming in their answers. Shaw has seized on an opening we can use, and I thought Mary might have been able to slip close to them and overhear any unguarded conversation."

Hannah set her hands on her hips. First her father had taken Timmy to an examination, and now Wycliff was asking Mary to assist with questioning? This alarming trend of asking others to do what Hannah wished to do needed to be nipped in the bud. "Why did you not ask me? It is my particular talent to speak to the females in any investigation."

Wycliff glanced at her from under dark brows. "Because it would not be appropriate. I am referring to the courtesans at La Perfumeria."

"Oh." Hannah turned to Frank. "Take Mary to the kitchen, please, and see that she has a cup of tea to revive her."

Carrying the maid as though she weighed nothing, he nodded and with slow, ponderous steps, left the room. Barnes trotted behind them like some rear guard.

"Two of our victims frequented that establishment prior to displaying symptoms of being fed upon. The courtesan called Penelope is known to bite her patrons, but I cannot ascertain whether she is truly a vampyre or some other form of creature. The owner is coy and merely says her ladies will be anything I want for the right price." Wycliff let go of the mantel to pace. As he walked, he ran a hand through his dark locks, further torturing a tuft. At that moment

Hannah noticed the resemblance of his hair to his smokey fur.

Hannah sought a topic of conversation while she pondered if she were brave enough to offer herself in Mary's stead. "I have often wondered why vampyres do not decay. Doctor Husom attributes it to the original consumption of Prometheus' liver—a trace might still flow through their blood." Blood was intolerable to the Afflicted. Her parents had tried a more liquid diet to see if that staved off the process of decomposition, but such experiments had failed. "Never before have we had access to one, to study them."

"Have you considered adopting a man's fashion in order to regularly visit Brae and examine him? Or it might be easier to inter him at the Repository for closer inspection," Wycliff murmured.

"Oh, brilliant idea!" Hannah met his gaze to find humour simmering in the dark depths. "You mock me."

"Not at all. I merely strive to feed your curiosity. But this discussion doesn't solve my current problem." He studied the clock as though seeking an answer from Father Time.

"Yes, it does. I shall offer myself as a maid." She steeled her backbone. Then a horrid thought struck her. *Maid* wasn't a euphemism for some deviant act in a brothel, was it? "I would simply serve tea or dust a dresser, wouldn't I?"

"I cannot ask this of you. A lady should never set foot in such a place." He stalked closer and took her hand in his.

"I think my chances of being seen and recognised are rather slim. But if you are concerned, my mother might have a temporary enchantment that can make me appear more like Mary." Now that she had made up her mind to infiltrate the sporting house, a tinge of excitement crept through her at her first act of subterfuge.

"Only if you are sure. Your assistance would be greatly appreciated." His thumb stroked over her knuckles.

A bolt of bravery shot through Hannah. "Does this mean you would owe me a token of affection?"

Heat flared in his eyes and her throat became parched. "I do believe I would," he murmured.

She tucked that information away for later. "How will I gain admittance as a maid?" While Hannah had no objection to serving tea or dusting, she wanted to ensure there weren't other tasks a maid in a brothel would be expected to perform.

"Shaw has intelligence that two of the maids have left due to being frightened by the panther shifter. An agency is sending a new girl to La Perfumeria and we can insert you as the replacement maid, if you could be ready by this afternoon?"

"I will confer with Mother. I am sure she can whip something up in time." Her bravery fleeing with every step, Hannah sought out her mother.

The mage concocted a spell that would overlay Hannah's features with those of Mary, and vice versa, for a short period of time. Each woman was given a bracelet to wear, plaited from the hair of the other.

Mary's bottom lip trembled and she looked close to tears as Hannah tied the plait around her wrist. "Will this steal my soul?"

Hannah clasped her hand. "No, of course not. This will allow me to be a maid for an afternoon and you, Mary, will be the lady, should anyone call."

Her eyes widened and she glanced to Frank, who loomed beside her. "I'll be a proper lady for the afternoon?"

"Why of course you will, Mary. Would you like tea in the front parlour while you put your feet up?" Seraphina asked.

A shy smile broke over the maid's face. "Oh, yes, milady. That would be grand."

"That is settled, then. Hannah will be set to work at La Perfumeria and Mary will have the afternoon off drinking tea and eating scones. Perhaps Frank could pay you a visit, like a proper gentleman caller?" Seraphina suggested.

The giant nodded and Mary blushed. With domestic matters in hand, Hannah left to complete her disguise.

On the way through the kitchen, Hannah glanced at herself in the glass of a cabinet and gasped. Mary's face looked back at her, although the eyes remained her own. She straightened her spine as she embarked on a new type of adventure—cleaning in a house of ill repute. No matter what her imagination conjured, she couldn't see its being any worse than cleaning up her father's laboratory after an autopsy on a bloated corpse. She hoped for far less bodily fluids and possibly a glimpse of the panther shifter.

Wycliff helped her into the carriage and sat opposite. He clenched the fingers of one hand against his knee, the other he held to his mouth as he chewed on his knuckle. His gaze remained fixed out the window on the fields beyond.

While nervous as to what she might encounter, Hannah didn't hold any real fear for either herself or her reputation. She pondered what to say to allay his concerns.

After some deliberation, she began, "I remember the first time we met, in the parlour of the house. I wore my old canvas apron with bloodstains on it from the autopsy my father had just conducted."

A sigh ran through his form and the clenched hand relaxed against his thigh. He turned to regard her and the tiniest smile hovered at the corner of his mouth. "You seek to reassure me about the task I have thrust upon you, when no gently bred woman should set foot in such a place."

"Due to my parents, I believe my eyes are somewhat more open than those of other young women of my acquaintance." She had placed her hands inside a cadaver's stomach cavity to remove organs. She couldn't conjure a horror that would make her squeamish.

His long fingers rapped on his knee. "But I am not

sending you into a slaughterhouse. There will be sights and...sounds...to which you should not be exposed. I am not altogether comfortable with your undertaking this task."

Hannah reached across and stilled his hand. "I am familiar with the human form and I am not so easily shocked. I will keep my ears and eyes focused on discerning whether or not a vampyre is part of the establishment."

He squeezed her hand. "I will not be far away, should you need my help. I have the mage silver ring from Barnes should you need to alert me urgently via your mother. I have asked if she could craft one for me and if it would be possible to create a way for us to signal each other. That would be more efficient for future investigations."

Hannah stared at him. Her mother had undertaken the intensive task of brewing enough mage silver in the event he requested one. That he now wanted such a ring meant he considered himself part of their family. The thought bloomed through her in unexpected ways, and she turned to stare out the window before he saw the wave of emotion behind her eyes.

Once they reached their destination, Wycliff issued a few brief instructions and then curled his hands around the edge of the seat, as though to stop himself from jumping out after her.

Hannah approached the back of the house and found it bustling with activity. A maid hauled baskets loaded with dirty linens that were placed against a wall, no doubt for the laundry service to collect. Another used a paddle to beat carpets dangling over a line. Voices called out, shouted, and sang. Men swept out the stables at the rear, waiting to offer rest to the horses of the men who visited.

She drew a deep breath and stepped over the open threshold into the large kitchen. A quick glance showed the woman in charge, dressed almost entirely in black, with a crisp apron over the top and her hair tucked up under a snowy cap. She issued orders to two young women.

"Are you from the agency?" she called to Hannah.

Remembering her manners, Hannah bobbed a curtsey. "Yes, ma'am."

The housekeeper gestured to the other women. "Excellent. You can help these two upstairs. That lot take forever to get ready and their breakfast is getting cold."

Breakfast? It was near two in the afternoon and the courtesans were only rising now? They kept the same hours as the most indolent nobles.

Wide-eyed, Hannah nodded. A heavy tray laden with covered dishes was thrust into her hands.

"I'm Faith, that there is Sarah." Faith picked up another tray with a large teapot wearing a knitted cosy in bright pink.

"I'm Mary," Hannah whispered and offered a shy smile.

"Follow us and try not to drop anything if you get

startled," Sarah said, using a towel to protect her hands as she picked up a large kettle of hot water.

Up the stairs and along a corridor, she followed the others. A young boy ran ahead and opened doors for them, since they all had their hands full. At their destination, Hannah stepped into a boudoir unlike anything she had ever seen. The walls were clad in striped wallpaper of buttery yellow and cream, with a delicate line of shimmering gold.

Four women lounged on chaises in diaphanous robes. Unbound hair tumbled around their shoulders in what could have been a painted scene of the gods at rest on Olympus.

"About time—I'm starved," a blonde woman yelled in a voice with a Cockney accent.

"New girl?" A dark gaze drilled into Hannah. With black hair and a dark complexion, the woman's gown of blood red suited her perfectly.

"Yes, ma'am." Hannah bobbed a curtsey.

"Are you easily scared?" the stern woman asked.

"No, ma'am." She shook her head. Far better that Wycliff had sent her instead of Mary, if this was to be the first question everyone asked. They would have learned nothing if the sensitive maid had passed out on the floor.

"We'll see." The woman stood and dropped her robe to reveal her naked form.

Nakedness didn't scare Hannah and objectively, she noted the woman's perfect figure with a good length of leg, sweeping waist, and pert breasts that the specimens in anatomy books all possessed.

Hannah had proceeded to lay out the dishes on the low table when a shimmer caught her eye. A soft mist enveloped the other woman's form, growing thicker until it obscured her from view. Then the dark shadow dropped to the carpet and in its place, a gleaming black panther stared at her. It opened its mouth and roared, exposing long, sharp canines.

"Oh, how marvellous," Hannah murmured, and she took a step forward.

The other women burst out laughing. The chilly blonde named Penelope called, "This one is not scared of you, Louise. Now change back before you shed everywhere. You know your fur makes me sneeze and I don't want a blotchy face and red nose for this evening."

The strange mist obscured Louise's form once more and when it dissipated, the naked woman stood in the middle of the carpet. She picked up a piece of toast and walked back to her chaise. Faith held out the robe for her to slide her arms through the sleeves. "Better to find out on the first day. So many of these maids are such fragile things they faint everywhere. You'd think they were bred to be ladies."

"Hang those up, but anything stained goes out to be laundered." Penelope gestured to a pile of discarded clothing draped over the back of a chair.

Hannah picked up a white silk gown with a delicate

embroidered edge of roses. The workmanship rivalled any gown she might find hanging in Lizzie's wardrobe. An inspection found the garment free of any *stains*, so Hannah found a hanger and wedged it in among numerous other fine dresses. The chemise and under-things most definitely needed to go out for laundering.

As Hannah took the dirty clothing to place in a basket by the door, she spotted something that did arrest her steps. A pair of gleaming fangs sat on a dresser. A loop of wire joined them together.

"Don't mind my teeth. Some gents like to be nibbled upon," Penelope called.

Hannah balled up the clothes and deposited them before turning to the courtesan with wide eyes. "Are you like one of those French vampyres?"

Louise cackled. "She's not undead, but her tricks like it when she lies still and does the fainting virgin routine."

Penelope threw a cushion at her friend. "Those were modelled after a real vampyre's teeth, I'll have you know. They are quite sharp and can bite deep. Some of those toffs pay extra if they think I'm drinking their blood."

Hannah wrinkled her nose. Drinking blood struck her as rather unsafe. Who knew what diseases a person's blood might harbour? She couldn't imagine what men found appealing about it. "I don't under-stand men and their fancies."

The women laughed. "You will after working here for a while."

Hannah and the other maids set to and tidied the room, put away the clothing, and dusted everything. Then they carried the baskets of laundry back down the stairs. Hannah went last, to leave her load next to the others. When the other maids walked back inside, she glanced around to ensure no one watched, and then scurried away.

She walked quickly to where the carriage waited along the road and climbed inside.

"Are you unharmed?" Wycliff took her hands and studied her intently, as though he thought she might be mortally wounded.

"I am well, and I can answer one question, although it raises more. Penelope is not a vampyre. She possesses a set of sharp fake canines that she informs me are capable of piercing the skin. Some of her visitors pay extra for her to sup upon them." The carriage rocked as it set off and Hannah leaned into the padding at her back.

"Blast." Wycliff let go of her hands and let the window down to lean an elbow on the narrow ledge. "She could have made the marks upon Burroughs or Stoneleigh, then."

"But she could not have drained two full-grown men," Hannah objected. "Quite apart from the fact it would have made her very ill. The level of exsanguina-tion we discovered would have entailed their being hung upside down with a major artery slit. And there was no evidence of that."

"So, either she had some other means to remove the

blood from their veins, or we're looking for someone else."

"If this is a common fantasy of some men, possibly our murderer is targeting Penelope's callers?" Hannah stared at her husband as a chilling thought crossed her mind. He wouldn't bare his throat, would he, to aid their enquiry?

As though reading her thoughts, he flashed her a smile. "Don't fret. I've no intention of wasting money to have her chew on me just to see if another waits to finish me off outside."

1 8

As THE AFTERNOON drew on toward dusk and birds chatted on their way to their evening roosts, Wycliff stood before the large fabric-covered board propped on the chair rail in his study. Handwritten notes were pinned alongside the drawings Hannah had made of the puncture wounds found on Burroughs and Stoneleigh. In her neat script, she had noted the exact measurements. Another pinned sheet contained the list of places the two men had visited prior to falling ill and their known associates, with red thread connecting the commonalities.

He had found one vampyre, but the man didn't appear to have either the opportunity or the motive. Especially since he maintained his own larder. Their questioning had revealed all the parties were indeed voluntary and the tailor didn't avail himself of any person more than once in a month. The person Wycliff had thought might be their bloodsucker had turned out to be a rather good actress with a set of fake fangs. Prometheus, the oldest vampyre in the world, had neither fangs nor an appetite for blood.

"What am I missing?" he murmured as his gaze roamed the notes and scraps of paper.

Hannah's pursuit of another method to drain a person had likewise failed to find the clue he needed. Her father eagerly experimented with leeches, but they left quite different marks. Not to mention the victims would have been covered in the slimy things. Nor was there such a creature as a human-sized leech shifter. Although he supposed vampyres should be classified as giant leeches.

The time had come for a fresh look at the evidence, and that meant setting aside his preoccupation with finding an undead assassin. Rather than focusing on *who* had killed the men, he would dig deeper into *why*. They had been targeted for a reason; he had only to find the strand that led to the motive.

There was one person who raised his hackles at whom he wanted a closer look—Baron Medwin. There was a possibility that someone among his guests might have taken to dining on nobles. He wanted to ask who else had attended during the evenings when Burroughs and Stoneleigh were present.

He found Hannah in one of her favourite spots— curled up in the library window seat, with the puppy asleep beside her. She set aside her work as he entered and greeted him with a smile.

The puppy stirred and jumped down to rush over

to sniff his boots. Wycliff picked up the spaniel and patted her head. "I intend to visit Medwin again, if you have time to accompany me?"

"Of course. I have a pot of Mother's salve that I wish to deliver to him. When did you wish to go?" She laughed as the puppy squirmed in his arms and attempted to lick his chin.

He tucked Sheba by his hip, where her tongue couldn't reach his face. "If we left in an hour or so, we could talk to him before his evening begins. I thought, perhaps, we might dine in London for a change? Sir Manly gave me a recommendation for a club that allows women if they are accompanied by their husbands. He said it had a pleasant atmosphere, good food, and a most excellent violinist. We are welcome to avail ourselves of his usual table." He added the offer of supper on impulse. He had enjoyed their quiet meals in the tavern when travelling in the countryside recently, and thought to replicate the experience. A meal under the constant watch of her parents sometimes left him on edge, as though he were a schoolboy sent to the headmaster's office for an unknown infraction.

Her eyes widened. "That sounds lovely. I must change."

"I'll take Sheba down to Timmy." He left the library with his wriggly passenger and sought out the lad. Then he walked out to the stables, where he found Old Jim and Frank cleaning harnesses in companionable silence. "I need the carriage around front in one hour and we'll be in London for a few hours."

"Right-o, my lord. If you don't mind, Frank here will take the reins. My bones are getting a bit old for sitting out in the cold and he don't seem to notice it," Old Jim said.

Wycliff nodded and when he led Hannah out of the house as twilight fell, Frank stood by the carriage wearing a Garrick coat that made him look even bulkier and more menacing. He closed the door upon them and the carriage lurched to one side as he climbed up to the driver's seat and they set off for London.

At the baron's residence, instead of being shown to the drawing room as on their previous visit, Hannah and Wycliff were shown through to the billiards room near the back of the house. Except it was a billiards room no more, but a small world contained within the confines of a room.

The green felt covering the billiards table gave way to a garden of tiny plants with flowers no bigger than a thumbnail. Miniature oak and birch stood no taller than a foot. A pond the size of a man's palm held silvery water and a diminutive duck paddled upon it. The other end of the table bore what appeared to be a house with no walls. Different rooms were denoted by various types of flooring. Lush carpets outlined a boudoir with a four-poster bed. A parlour had wooden floors with striped rugs. Black and white tiles adorned a bathroom with a copper tub. Lights floated above the furniture, held in place by faint slivers of magic.

Baron Medwin leaned on one side of the table, talking to the tiny people upon it. "No, no, no. Stop laughing. This is supposed to be a tragedy." He glanced up as they entered and pushed away from the table to bow. "Lord and Lady Wycliff. To what do I owe this honour?"

Hannah's attention fixed on the wooden puppets and she moved to the side of the table. Four marionettes strolled among the gardens. Two others sat upon a chaise in the house. They were dressed in Georgian costumes, the men with lavishly embroidered coats reminiscent of a peacock's iridescent greens and blues, with flourishes of lace at neck and wrist. The women wore delicate pinks and yellows complete with panniers and sackback dresses that flowed behind them.

Wycliff glanced at the tiny actors and then turned to Medwin. "I have a few more questions about Burroughs. I assume you have heard that Stoneleigh died under similar circumstances? Both of them were known to come here to watch your shows."

Tearing her gaze from the puppets that moved with no strings, Hannah dug into her reticule and pulled out a jar. "As I mentioned during our last visit, here is the salve from my mother that you are most welcome to try."

Today the baron went without his enchantment to hide his disfigured face. Half his face pulled into a smile and crinkled the edge of the undamaged blue eye. He took the pot and held it up to stare at the faint pearlized gleam coming from the contents. "Thank you, Lady Wycliff. You are most thoughtful. I shall apply it this evening." He set the pot on the edge of the billiards table and gestured to the tableau. "As you can see, my actors are awake and stretching their legs before tonight's performance."

Hannah stared at the performers intently and Wycliff wondered what she discerned about them. Some sort of magic must make the things move and it would ripple over her skin. He made a mental note to ask when they were back in the carriage.

"Do they speak?" Wycliff asked.

"Yes, in their own tongue." Baron Mcdwin reached out and tapped the hand of a young man with dark brown hair that curled around his face. "We have visitors. Say hello."

The puppet took off his hat and swept a courtly bow in Hannah's direction. He made a trilling noise, not unlike a bird. Around him, the other puppets turned and either bowed or curtseyed, each adding their unique voice to his greeting until they formed a twilight chorus.

The odd birdsong wrapped around Wycliff and vibrated through his body. He wanted to hear more and found himself stepping closer. He fixed on the movement of carved mouths as they sang. Then, aware he had nearly fallen under the spell of wooden toys, he shook his head to regain his focus.

Hannah seemed entranced and leaned farther over the table. A tiny flower burst open and a puff of luminescent yellow pollen drifted upward. She sneezed and placed a hand over her face, while with the other she fumbled in her reticule. "My apologies. I didn't realise I was so close to a flower."

"Allow me." Baron Medwin produced a handkerchief with a flourish and held it out to her before Wycliff could offer his.

"Thank you," she managed to say before another sneeze, and she turned her back to blow her nose.

"I require a list of the other guests present when Stoneleigh and Burroughs were here," Wycliff said. He extracted his notebook and pencil while the baron searched his memory for names.

"Hmm... Enderley, Thornton, that duke who always attracts a certain type of enterprising young woman." He winked, but the damaged eye stared with its muddy gaze. He rattled off a dozen more names and then shook his head. "Those are all that I can recollect. My usual guests will be attending tonight. If there is anyone I forgot, I will be sure to pass the name along."

Wycliff tucked the notebook away and cast a glance around the room. The baron's staff laid out drinks and fruit on sideboards and moved chairs into position in readiness for the nobles who would watch the puppets.

Hannah shot him a look not unlike that of the puppy when she was left behind. Her request to stay was clear.

"We have other plans, Hannah," he murmured and offered her his arm.

"Another time, Lady Wycliff. Tonight's performance contains rather...indelicate scenes, not appropriate for a gentlewoman such as yourself." The baron bowed and gestured for them to precede him out the door. There, Hannah extended the handkerchief, but the baron waved it away. "Keep it, until you can return to watch my associates perform."

On the street, Wycliff gave Frank the address of the club and helped Hannah up into the carriage. They had only a short journey to their next destination. Sir Manly had passed over his reservation to Wycliff and told him not to worry about the bill. While he was grateful, Wycliff suspected the dinner was in lieu of payment for all Hannah's work to assist him. In which case he would make sure they enjoyed the wine cellar and had dessert.

Frank deposited them outside the club and Wycliff told him to wait in the mews until he was sent for. Inside, the address exuded a calm peacefulness. The dark panelled walls were softened by carpets in lush greens and blues. The dining room had been set out with a dozen round tables, each seating only two diners. Draped in white linen and set with a silver service, an enclosed lantern flickered in the middle of each table. The high-backed chairs were upholstered in a brocade of blue shades. In one corner, a man played a violin and the music drifted around the room much like the song of Medwin's puppets.

"What a charming place," Hannah said as they followed the steward to their table.

Wycliff held out her chair before taking his seat across from her, where the server flicked out the linen napkin and draped it over his knee. "I thought it might be a pleasant change, although not as lively as the tavern."

The closed atmosphere created intimacy between the diners. Conversations were conducted in hushed tones, as though great secrets, or affections, were confided. Most tables were occupied by one gentleman and a lady companion; only one hosted two men, their heads bent close together.

"Did you detect the magic bringing the puppets to life?" he asked after the server had poured the wine.

Hannah reached for her glass, but it hovered by her lips as she gathered her thoughts. After a small sip, she placed the glass back on the table. "Yes and no. My skin tingled with the wash of magic at play in the room, but it seemed insufficient for the size of the enchantment in use. It could even have been from the baron's locket, as it felt the same."

Wycliff frowned. "But surely the dolls are ensorcelled in some way? We know he is not an aftermage and therefore can't be controlling them directly himself."

She ran a finger along the edge of the menu. "It is possible they use a type of magic I am unfamiliar with. I shall consult with Mother tomorrow."

The server took their order and disappeared again on silent feet. Murmurs of conversation rose and fell around them, and the violin music drifted sweetly over the room.

"We are still no closer to uncovering who is responsible. Both men did owe a sum to Brae, but it didn't seem significant enough to kill them for." Wycliff ran through possible suspects in a hushed tone, so as not to alarm their fellow diners.

"Not when you consider how solicitous he is to his patrons. Do you think the duke has had a change in his affections toward Lizzie?" Hannah blurted out, suddenly changing the direction of the conversation.

"A change in his affections? No. What makes you ask?" Wycliff brought to mind his private interview with the duke, wherein he had expressed his unfashionable love and devotion to his bride-to-be.

Hannah glanced around and leaned over her plate. "Lizzie feels he has grown rather distant of late and worries his affections have lessened."

Wycliff hid a smile behind his wine glass. Hannah was a mother hen where her friend was concerned, always making sure the other woman's life ran smoothly. "I can assure you, he loves her and she commands his full loyalty. He is a man with many matters to handle and who takes on much responsibility. I suspect he is merely tired. Their time abroad will see him fully restored."

She let out a sigh. "I told her much the same thing, but thank you for venturing a man's opinion on the subject."

They enjoyed a most pleasant meal, including an iced dessert that used a magical process to freeze cream and sugars. A warmth spread through Wycliff as he helped Hannah up into the carriage. She settled in a corner and watched him through half-lidded eyes. As they set off toward home, he wondered if tonight might be the occasion to ask if he could visit her bedchamber. But how to word such a request?

If he blurted it out in the carriage and she balked, or confessed to not being ready yet, that would create an awkward atmosphere for the remaining miles home. What would a suave wolf do? Ewan Shaw would never risk a chilly half-hour ride back to the house if she declined such a request. He would wait for the perfect moment, when intimacy wrapped itself around them. Such as when they parted company on the stairs. Alone in the silent house, he would seek a good-night kiss and murmur his offer against her lips. Yes. That seemed a most excellent plan.

When they arrived in Westbourne Green, he discovered one major flaw in his idea. Hannah had fallen asleep, lulled by the rocking of the carriage, and she did not even stir when Frank opened the door and peered within. The giant glanced at Wycliff and before he could whisper an objection, the other man had reached in and picked up Hannah as though he plucked the puppy off a sofa.

Wycliff let out a frustrated sigh and followed. He would have preferred to play the gallant and carry his wife in his arms.

Mary met them at the door. "Bless me," she murmured on seeing her mistress slumbering in the monster's embrace. She waved a hand to shoo Wycliff away as though he were a curious chicken. "You go off to bed, my lord. Frank can carry her up and I'll tuck her into bed."

In one dismissive gesture, all Wycliff's romantic plans were scuttled. Perhaps their marriage *was* destined to remain one in name only.

19

Hannah awoke the next morning and stretched her arms over her head. As she reviewed her lovely evening with her husband, she remembered how it had ended. "Oh, no," she gasped and sat bolt upright. She glanced around as though she half expected to find she still slept in the carriage.

"What is it, my lady?" Mary stood by the wardrobe, selecting a gown for the day.

"I fell asleep on Wycliff. What must he think of me?" He disliked idle chatter, so perhaps he wouldn't judge the silence of slumber too harshly. It had been the most wonderful supper and unusually for her, she had indulged in two glasses of wine. It would appear that alcohol put her to sleep faster than warm milk.

"I imagine he will think you were tired, ma'am. There's no need to fret. You were carried ever so tenderly inside and put to bed, then I changed you into your nightgown." A soft expression fell over Mary's face and she clutched a gown to herself.

Tenderly? That made heat prickle over Hannah's skin. She imagined Wycliff cradling her to his chest as he bore her through the house. Perhaps she nestled her face into his neck and his aroma settled over her like a secure blanket. In her mind, she saw him laying her out on the bed like the prince setting Snow White on her forest bed. Had he kissed her lips before he left? She touched her fingertips to them, but couldn't tell.

As she stretched out, she discovered the puppy, who had crept onto the bed during the night and curled up next to her. Instead of heated kisses from her husband, Hannah's morning began with joyful kisses from the spaniel.

"Frank is ever so gentle." Mary draped the green-and-brown-striped gown over the screen in the corner of the room by the fire.

"Frank?" Hannah dropped her feet to the ground and Sheba jumped off the bed.

"Yes. Frank carried you. He is the strongest man and most tender soul I have ever met." Mary walked to the dresser to add undergarments and short stays to the items flung over the screen.

Hannah's mood deflated like a soufflé pulled from the oven too soon. It would seem that Mary's romance with Frank had made greater advances than Hannah's with her own husband.

"You seem rather taken by Frank. I hope he behaves honourably toward you," Hannah said as she stepped behind the screen and pulled her nightgown up over her head. Love bloomed in the oddest gardens, but the flowers were no less beautiful.

"Oh, yes, my lady. He's a bit too proper at times. Sometimes all a woman wants is a kiss from the fellow she adores." Mary's voice came from the other side of the screen.

There was a sentiment Hannah shared. As unlikely as the match might appear between maid and monster, no one could doubt the affection between them. That made another worry appear in her mind. Could Mary marry Frank, if he made such an offer? He possessed a heartbeat, unlike the Afflicted, so technically wasn't dead. But he had died. That led her to wonder what Wycliff would find if he viewed Frank and Barnes with his hellhound's vision. There was an experiment to try when he had the free time.

When Hannah walked into the breakfast room, she found Wycliff alone. He rose as she took her seat and fidgeted with her napkin. "I wanted to apologise, Wycliff, for falling asleep on the journey home. That was rude of me, but I fear the wine made me sleepy."

He stared at her with an odd light in his eyes, as though he might chastise her, then he huffed a quiet laugh. "Entirely understandable. You know my preference for silence and it made for a rather quiet ride home."

Hannah grinned over the rim of her cup. "I shall assume that I didn't snore, then?"

"I assure you, madam, a husband would never

betray his wife's confidence by revealing that information." He winked and then snapped open the newspaper.

Sir Hugh joined them, pushing Seraphina before him. "Good morning all!" he said as he positioned his wife at the table.

"How was your evening, you two?" Seraphina's voice was infused with a light mood and she wore a crown fashioned from intertwined peacock feathers and bound with silver.

"Baron Medwin's puppets were rehearsing when we visited. The billiards table has been converted into a marvellous landscape complete with a doll's house and garden. There was even a tiny duck paddling on a pond no bigger than my cup." No matter how hard Hannah had tried, she couldn't discern how the wooden dolls moved and talked. If she possessed any trace of magic, their secrets would have been revealed to her.

"What is your opinion of them, my dear? Are they mere wood, brought to life by an aftermage puppeteer, or are they ensorcelled dolls?" Seraphina tilted her head as she waited for her daughter's answer.

Hannah sipped her tea and gathered her thoughts. "I detected a faint magical trace in their presence. But the baron wears a miniature in a locket that he uses to hide his disfigurement. It is possible what I felt came from that."

She closed her eyes and recalled the exquisite forms that strolled the garden springing from the billiards table's green felt. Mentally, she compared them to the Punch and Judy shows of her childhood, but those were crude things with fat heads, and the puppeteer's hand manipulating events was obvious.

"The puppets must be some magical creation. Although I would have thought you'd have a greater reaction to them. Could they be gnomes in disguise?" Her mother laughed as she poured coffee for her husband.

Hannah snorted into her tea. "Mother. If you had only seen them. They are...breathtaking and of such pure beauty. Why, even our Lizzie would appear ordinary next to them. They are far too elegant and beautiful to be gnomes. But if they were such creatures, that might explain why I couldn't detect any magic in use."

Wycliff frowned over the top of the paper. "Why can't gnomes be elegant?"

"Very short. Dense bone structure," Sir Hugh said as he picked up his cutlery.

Wycliff's eyebrows shot up but he resisted asking the obvious question—how did Hannah's father know about the bone structure of gnomes? Shaking his head, he folded up the paper and turned his attention to breakfast.

Conversation shot around the table and after a lively meal, Hannah took hold of the bathchair and wheeled her mother to the library.

"Let us start our day by digging deeper into the background of Baron Medwin to see if we can find him hidden somewhere in the genealogies." Seraphina waved her hands and muttered under her breath.

The enormous tome with the current living descendants of mages wriggled free of its spot on the bookshelf and glided down to the desk. It landed with a plop, seemed to collect its breath, and then with a huff, flicked itself open.

"Let us see if I overlooked a love child or adoption, although it is rare for the book to be wrong." She held one hand over the pages and scanned the names with a gloved fingertip.

"Meanwhile, I shall resort to a less magical book." Hannah crossed to the bookshelves and scanned the titles. She plucked one free and turned back to her mother with a grin. "Debrett's."

The volume with its dark blue leather cover and gold embossed lettering detailed the peerage of England. Hannah scanned the entries, looking for Medwin. When she didn't find it, she started again.

"Problem?" Seraphina asked.

"Baron Medwin does not appear." She passed the book over to her mother for a second opinion.

"There is the possibility that it isn't an English title, but a European one," Seraphina said as she scanned the smaller volume.

Hannah waved to the enormous book that occupied most of the desk. "Similarly, he could be an aftermage, but recorded in the genealogies of another country."

Her mother closed Debrett's and handed it back. "Good point, Hannah. I shall put out the word to my European counterparts immediately, and see if they can uncover his name somewhere. Now, we must finalise things for the wedding. The enchantments are complete, whenever you are ready to take them to the Loburns' and position them in the ballroom and church."

At mention of the wedding, Hannah clutched Debrett's to her chest. She needed to talk to Lizzie about Harden, and hoped Wycliff's confirmation of the duke's devotion would allay her friend's concerns.

"Whatever has caused that sad face?" Seraphina wheeled her chair back from the desk and around the side.

"Oh, I was thinking of Lizzie. She has been worried of late about Harden and says he has become somewhat distant in recent days." Hannah slid the blue book into the waiting space on the shelf.

"And what did you think when you last saw him?" Seraphina summoned the large sheet of paper that contained the layout of the ballroom for the wedding dance.

"He looked tired, which I think is hardly surprising with all he is planning, and about to welcome a new duchess into his household. It will not be an easy transition—the staff have been without a mistress since his mother died." Hannah sat on the library floor at her mother's feet, and Sheba climbed into her lap. Hannah stroked the silken ears as the puppy rested across her knees.

"I am sure, as you say, that Harden has much to worry about at the moment, but for his own reasons, chooses not to burden his bride." Another, smaller sheet of paper joined the first. This contained the more intimate delights that would unfold in the small church as Lord Loburn walked Lizzie down the aisle.

"If Harden spoke to her, it would allay her fears. Poor thing was convinced he no longer loves her and wishes to be released from the engagement. I asked Wycliff last night and he is of the opinion that the duke's affections have not wavered." Hannah paused and the puppy squirmed to remind her to keep up the attention.

"I imagine nerves have roused an unfounded concern for our Lizzie. The duke loves her most devotedly. Men are odd creatures. They bottle up all their feelings and prefer to be seen as brooding and tortured, rather than share the worries they harbour." Seraphina waved her hand and a single blush-pink rose petal appeared above her head and drifted into her palm.

Sheba decided the petting had stopped for too long and leapt up to lick Hannah's face. The spontaneous spaniel kiss made her smile. Rather different to the slow kiss Wycliff had shared with her in the glade. That day already seemed an eternity ago, if it had even happened at all. Perhaps she'd dreamed the encounter. Although she could never have dreamt of how he had suffered as his men were slaughtered around him, nor of his despair as he waited for death to take him.

"Speaking of tortured...how are things with Wycliff?" Seraphina rolled her hands together and the petal disappeared, to be replaced by a short, plaited length of rope.

Hannah hugged Sheba, which resulted in more puppy kisses. "There is a man long used to bottling things up. Although we are taking steps along the road to sharing our secrets."

Seraphina waved the piece of rope at the spaniel, who jumped to her feet to snatch one end. "All things are revealed by time," the mage murmured.

AFTER BREAKFAST, Wycliff rode for London to talk to the other people who had attended Baron Medwin's evenings and was gone most of the day. As afternoon lengthened, Hannah sat out on the terrace with the others. It had become a regular thing to have Timmy catch the chickens and ensure their feathered friends were healthy. Everyone enjoyed the fun. Barnes helped, while Hannah held on to Sheba to stop the puppy from chasing the chickens and upsetting their delicate equilibriums. Mary and Frank sat to one side and laughed.

Wycliff's sleek black mare came around the side of the house. Her husband jumped to the ground and nodded a greeting. Then horse and rider disappeared into the shaded interior of the stables. Some time later he emerged, skirted the edge of the action, and sat next to Hannah on a wide step.

"Did you discover anything in London?" Hannah asked as Timmy clutched a chicken and closed his eyes.

"Very little. I doubt the nobles I spoke to collectively contained as much intelligence as that chicken." He waved to the placid bird in Timmy's arms.

"That's the last one!" Timmy announced as he set the hen free to dash after her sisters.

Twilight reached out grey tendrils toward them and the sky dimmed above.

"Why don't you take Timmy to the kitchen, Mary? Tell Cook he may have a treat for his most excellent work," Seraphina called out.

The lad beamed as he skipped up the stairs ahead of Mary.

Hannah waited until both had disappeared into the house. Then she took Wycliff's hand and turned toward him. "Have you ever tried to look at Frank or Barnes with the hound's vision? It might assist us to know what you see."

He let out a breath and glanced at Barnes, intent on drawing what appeared to be a ship in the dirt. "I can try. I am practicing the partial shift and managed to alter my vision in Brae's shop without igniting the carpet."

Even the birds in the trees above fell silent as Wycliff breathed deep through his nostrils. His head shimmered and his hair floated around his face like smoke. When he opencd his eyes, Hannah swallowed a startled gasp. The red eyes of the hound looked out at her.

"What do you notice about Barnes?" she asked in a quiet tone.

He turned to where the disembodied hand roamed

across the dirt, stalking the puppy. "He has an odd glow. Not the golden tone that you have. This has a green tinge."

Hannah would turn that information over later—the different colour might be a clue to whatever formula Dalkeith had used. "Is his soul nearby, like you see with Mother?"

"No. He wanders alone." Wycliff turned his head to stare at Frank, off to one side. He stared for a long moment, then inhaled sharply and lowered his head. His shoulders heaved and his smoky hair settled back into its earthly form.

"Frank? Why don't you go find Mary and see how long supper will be?" Hannah said.

The large man's steps shook the terrace stairs as he climbed them into the house.

"What was it?" Hannah glanced from the house to Wycliff. Whatever could he have seen in Frank that had provoked such a reaction? They had all grown accustomed to his physical form, the angry scars, and his odd yellow eyes.

"He has the same green glow as Barnes, but it is confined to his torso and head. The rest..." He laced his fingers with Hannah's and stared at their joined hands. "There are *five souls*, Hannah. Attached to his body like phantom shackles at his arms and legs. I have seen it before with Beth, the woman slain by Dalkeith. The two others were attached to her by silver strands."

Hannah glanced up at her mother on the terrace proper, to ensure she had heard Wycliff's quiet words.

"They cannot rest or move on to the underworld. They have died, but parts of them live on and so their souls must remain with those pieces," the mage murmured.

Hannah thought through the implications for Frank, forever attached to the souls of those used in his construction. What of those souls—did they suffer an eternal torment being unable to seek eternal peace after their deaths? Although at least they lived a quiet existence with the Miles family.

"Do you think he knows?" Hannah whispered.

"The Afflicted who tried such a transplant were tormented by the old memories of the limb used. While he may not be aware of the souls, he most probably shares the memories attached to the limbs given him," Sir Hugh said.

Wycliff stood and held out a hand to Hannah.

"Even if he endures such torment, he keeps his gentle heart. Yet others who suffer far less let rage consume them." Hannah slipped her hand into the crook of Wycliff's elbow and pondered the differences in how people let circumstances dictate their actions.

20

AFTER DINNER, and for the first evening in many days, the family retired to the drawing room as night blanketed the countryside. Wycliff played chess with Sir Hugh, both combatants bent over the board. Seraphina read from a book so large it was propped up on a desk. Hannah curled up with Sheba and a fashionable novel about the aristocracy.

The loud rapping at the window interrupted the quiet. Wycliff glanced up. The noise was oddly familiar.

"Hannah, why is a giant owl trying to gain entry to the house?" her father asked from his chair as Wycliff stalked over and flung open the window.

"This is Higgs, from the Ministry," Wycliff answered as the creature perched on the windowsill. He plucked the envelope from the owl's beak, tore it open, and scanned the contents.

Seraphina leaned forward over the book, peering at

the enormous owl. "It seems Sir Manly has found a far more efficient means of communication than my little weather cubes. An oversized barn owl at the window does rather catch one's attention."

Wycliff thanked Higgs and waved the owl away before shutting the window. Then he sought Hannah's gaze. "We are summoned immediately. All of us—Enderley is near death."

Sir Hugh pushed his chair back and stood. "I'll fetch my bag and Timmy. Hannah, could you rouse Frank to hitch up the carriage, please?"

Hannah set aside her book, but paused at the door. "Do you think we should ask Doctor Husom for his assistance? I think he might have a unique insight into these deaths. Quite apart from his origins, he does possess a brilliant mind honed by millennia of research."

Wycliff considered the idea of seeking the assistance of the man who had fathered the entire race of vampyres. "Ask Old Jim to harness the buggy, while Frank does the carriage. We will need both vehicles for that many of us, and one of us can take the buggy to fetch Husom."

She nodded, and set off at a trot to find Frank.

"Enderley? Who follows Burroughs and Stoneleigh?" Seraphina froze with her hands on the wheels of her chair.

Wycliff paused, about to follow his wife. Something in the mage's tone made his hackles rise. "Yes. Do you know them?"

Her fingers tapped against the wheels. "The names are known to me. But these are young men, yes?"

From his estimation, they were all of the same generation, although they did not move in the same circles. "I would say all three would be about my age. Do you know something that is relevant to this investigation?"

Seraphina shook her head. "A mere coincidence, I am sure. The names remind me of something from long ago. But you must go—leave me to my thoughts."

They assembled in the courtyard and Wycliff made a decision. The physician was needed most urgently to tend the dying man. His investigation could wait until the man's fate was decided one way or the other. "Hannah, you go with your father and Timmy directly to Enderley. I will take the buggy and fetch Husom."

They parted ways once they turned out of the drive. Wycliff urged the cob onward to a canter as he headed for Chelsea. He only slowed the horse to a walk as they neared the doctor's residence. He glanced at the windows as he jumped down. A light burned in the front room, but no light escaped the attic laboratory—not that he could see in unless he climbed onto the roof and peered through the skylights.

Wycliff rapped sharply and hoped the doctor was downstairs this evening. He was about to knock again when the lock rattled and the door opened.

"Lord Wycliff," Doctor Husom said, peering over the tops of his spectacles. "I assume you are here on an urgent matter, since you are not renowned for social visits."

"Enderley is near death from possible blood loss and Sir Hugh was summoned urgently. I came to fetch you, if you would give a second opinion on his condition?" He bounced on his toes, keen to be on his way again.

"Of course. Let me fetch my coat and bag. I shan't be more than five minutes." True to his word, the doctor reappeared in less than five minutes, an old coat around his shoulders, carrying a large black leather bag.

Wycliff urged the cob along the roads and they soon found Enderley's smart address. He left the horse to the care of a stable lad and the butler ushered them through the house and up the stairs. This time, they were admitted to Enderley's bedchamber and not his adjoining parlour.

In the middle of the bed, Enderley lay so still that Wycliff wondered if they were too late and he had passed already. Then he drew a shallow breath. Hannah stood to one side of the room. Sir Hugh held the man's wrist and searched for a pulse while Timmy rested his hands over Enderley's chest.

The young lad glanced up at his teacher. "His heart is struggling, Sir Hugh, but it's not quite done for yet."

Doctor Husom strode across the room and stopped at the bedside. Timmy jumped out of the way and stood next to Hannah. He stared down at the dying man and a frown pulled his brows closer together. "You think a vampyre did this?"

Sir Hugh lowered the victim's arm to the coverlet. "With complete certainty? No. But he exhibits all the signs of extreme blood loss. Timmy here found the veins are close to dried up."

Husom placed his black leather bag on the chaise at the end of the bed. Then he stripped off his jacket and flung it down. Next, he cracked open the bag and pulled out a length of dark red tubing that resembled intestines. "There is one thing we may try, but I do not know what result it might have."

"What is that?" Wycliff asked, trying to make sense of the equipment.

"A transfusion of my blood. I can replenish what he has lost and it will not adversely affect me, as I will regenerate by morning." From the bag, he pulled out a bottle with two valves sticking out from either side of the lid.

"Will the process turn him into a vampyre?" Hannah stepped toward the bed.

Wycliff knew very little about how one vampyre created another. Lycanthropes and hellhounds used a bite that somehow infected the new creature. From what he could recall, vampyres required a more active exchange, where the fledgling consumed the blood of its creator.

Doctor Husom laid out the equipment on the bed, then rolled up the sleeve of his shirt. "That I cannot answer. I have never tried the procedure, only hypothesised that it might work in an extreme case of exsanguination. We can debate the possible effects while he dies, or try it and see if we can save him."

Sir Hugh picked up a leather roll containing needles and gestured Timmy over. Then he handed the lad two tourniquets. The bedroom resembled an operating room with the medical men huddled around the bedside. Wycliff was cast in the role of useless observer.

Hannah placed a chair next to the bed and the doctor sat. She exchanged a glance with her father. "Should we ask if he consents, given the risk?"

Wycliff snorted. Some fops enjoyed pretending they were vampyres. "He's a dandy—this is probably his darkest fantasy made real."

Hannah rested a hand on Wycliff's arm. "Someone should speak for him, surely, before he is irrevocably changed? Especially if he cannot speak for himself."

Her words rankled. No one had given him a choice. In hindsight, what would he have chosen? A quick end to his empty life, or anguish followed by an altered life with Hannah in it? He took her hand and turned it over to run his thumb across her palm. "To do so would unmask the doctor's true nature and, possibly, further alarm his family. It might also be false hope, if our efforts fail to save him."

Hannah glanced at Doctor Husom, who prepared the tubing to siphon off his blood and funnel it into Lord Enderley. A furrow ran across her brow.

"We do not have much time, Hannah. How he has cheated death for this long, I do not know, but I shall let you be our conscience in this matter." Sir Hugh met his daughter's gaze.

She made a decision and pulled her hand free of Wycliff's grasp. "What can I do?"

"If you assist Doctor Husom, I will find a vein in Lord Enderley." Sir Hugh gestured to the waiting tourniquet.

Hannah picked up the strap and looped it around Doctor Husom's upper arm. She pulled it tight, then tapped his inner elbow to encourage a vein to the surface. Needle in hand, she glanced up. "There may be a prick."

A smile broke over Husom's face. "For centuries I had my liver plucked out every day by a giant eagle. I think I can endure a needle in your gentle hands."

Wycliff paced as she slid the needle into the vein and attached the tubing to the end. Doctor Husom released the tourniquet and blood spurted along the tubing and trickled into the bottle.

With some effort, Sir Hugh undertook a similar procedure on the unresponsive lord. He muttered as he struggled to find the right spot to insert the needle. "Poor chap, his veins are collapsing." After a few moments he uttered a soft noise of satisfaction. "It's in."

"Attach the tubing. Time is of the essence and we can start the transfer immediately. You will need to use the plunger on the top to get it moving." Doctor Husom squeezed his hand into a fist.

The container held the ends of the two tubes and a pump in the lid would create the action necessary for one line to suck up the blood and deliver it to the drained man. Sir Hugh raised and lowered the metal lever. Wycliff couldn't look away as blood travelled up the second tube, and along its length. Inch by inch, it made its way to Enderley. After what seemed hours, the entire line filled and the doctor's immortal blood flowed into the patient.

"Now what?" Wycliff asked. He had kept out of the way of their work, but watched everything with a keen eye.

"We wait, and hope it works." With nothing more to do, Hannah returned to Wycliff's side and slipped her hand into his.

"I wish I had brought my notebook to record our findings," Husom muttered as he kept pumping his fist to keep blood flowing.

Wycliff pondered if they were doing the right thing. What if Lord Enderley arose as one of the undead? From what he observed of the other man, at least he had the requisite taste in fashion. The Ministry would need to institute some protocols for the blood-drinking creatures to follow. His idea of getting Unwin and Alder on to meeting their needs grew in merit. Perhaps he should ask about investing in the company first? An additional revenue stream would surely increase the value of their stock.

The clock ticked like an overloud heartbeat as Sir Hugh monitored both patients. A strange transference occurred as blood from one man entered the other—their appearances were likewise traded. Doctor Husom grew pale and gaunt, even as Lord Enderley's cheeks filled out and took on the bloom of health.

"By Jove, it's working, Husom! Timmy, why don't you try your gift now?" Sir Hugh rubbed his hands together in anticipation.

Timmy rested his hands on the sleeper's chest and closed his eyes. When he opened them again, he had a toothy grin. "He's out of danger, Sir Hugh. His heart is beating more regular-like and his veins aren't cracking anymore."

"Excellent. Let's take these lines out. Perhaps Doctor Husom would like a cup of tea and a biscuit to perk him up?" He gestured for his daughter to tend to the other doctor.

Wycliff recalled that Brae's male patrons preferred a brandy and marzipan after they had given their blood, but presumed tea and biscuits would have a similar effect.

Doctor Husom's eyelids fluttered and his breath seemed irregular in his chest. "No. Take me home. Do not be alarmed if I die on the journey. I will be well by morning."

Hannah removed the needle from the doctor's arm and applied one of her mother's spiderweb-backed bandages. He slumped in the chair and appeared about to fall. Despite his assurances, Wycliff didn't wish the man to die due to his efforts to save the noble. Even if it would be a temporary death and he would awaken in the morning. Was it an unpleasant experience? Or did Prometheus slip back and forth from death to life like a sleeper moving in and out of a dream?

With no other task to perform, Wycliff opened the bedroom door and sent the hovering footman to summon the family. The dowager Lady Enderley rushed to her son's bedside. Tears ran down her cheeks at the flush of colour in her son's face. "Thank you! Thank you!" she cried and then she took her son's hand and refused to let go.

Timmy and Hannah packed away the supplies. The younger Lady Enderley approached. "Is there anything we should do to assist this miraculous recovery?"

"Keep him rested and offer him bone broth if he desires it when he awakes," Hannah advised.

Wycliff's eyebrows shot up, but he kept silent. Enderley might prefer blood when he roused. What he needed in his soup bowl would depend on whether or not he possessed a pulse.

"Sir Hugh will return in the morning to examine him." He met his father-in-law's gaze.

Once they knew the effects of the transfusion, and if the blood used to save his life had turned him into an undead creature, they could decide what to tell Lord Enderley and his family. Meanwhile, Wycliff would be prepared to add a new entry in the Ministry's ledger.

"I will stay here at my dear boy's bedside," Lady Enderley said.

"Summon me if his condition worsens, but I think I can confidently say the worst is over." Sir Hugh patted the slumbering man's arm, below the wrapped bandages around his inner elbow.

"Let's get you into a carriage, Husom. Could you help me, Wycliff?" Sir Hugh put one of Doctor Husom's arms around his shoulder. Wycliff took the other side and the two men carried the limp Immortal between them.

Wycliff and Sir Hugh loaded Doctor Husom into the carriage. Then Wycliff helped Hannah up into the buggy. She took up the reins and Wycliff placed his hand over hers. "You were right in your suggested course of action, Hannah. Doctor Husom may have saved Enderley. Once he is awake, he may reveal the name of the person who did this to him."

She smiled and leaned down to kiss his cheek. "If it brings this investigation to a swift end, I will be most pleased."

He watched her drive off with Timmy beside her, before climbing into the carriage to see the prone doctor home. Once the investigation was brought to a close and her friend married, he had an idea percolating in his brain.

Never mind assignations on the staircase under the noses of her parents. Did he have the courage to take Hannah to his ancestral home and ask her to truly be his wife?

AT MIDAFTERNOON, they gathered in the library. Wycliff and Sir Hugh had visited Enderley earlier, and shared their findings.

"He is much restored—sitting up and eating breakfast," Sir Hugh said. "Bone broth, before you ask, Hannah. His digestive system does not appear to have any craving for blood. He also possesses a heartbeat. We will, of course, monitor him closely."

Relief washed through her that the actions of Doctor Husom had prised one person free of the murderer's actions.

"Unfortunately, he has no recollection of what happened. He said he felt tired, went to bed early, and woke up this morning wondering what all the fuss was about. Yet again we have no direction to follow." Wycliff stood by the fireplace and leaned against the mantel.

"I might be able to help there." Seraphina gestured to the library door as Mary burst in.

"Lady Loburn is here, my lady," she breathed and then stepped aside as Lizzie's mother strode into the room.

"Thank you for coming, Kitty." Seraphina held out her hands to her friend.

Lady Loburn kissed Seraphina's veiled cheek and then regarded each of them in turn as she stripped off her pelisse and matching hat and handed them off to Mary.

"Is this about the wedding?" Hannah asked. Her friend's mother only travelled out to them on rare occasions.

"In a way, yes. But I have information that may assist Wycliff's investigation." Lady Loburn clasped her hands together, her lips set in a grim line. She stared at Seraphina for a long time, as some unspoken conversation occurred between the two women. Then she let out a sigh. "You will forgive me if I start by going back in time. The full story from its inception may provide the clue you need to find the person responsible for these murders."

Everyone glanced at each other and held their silence. Lady Loburn began her story. "In 1760, a young George III came to the British throne. In accordance with a long-held tradition between our realms, a representative from the Fae court attended the coronation. They sent Princess Deryn, who, it transpired, became *intimately* acquainted with the new king in her brief time here."

Hannah swallowed a gasp and wished she could have seen the Fae delegation. It was well over fifty years since one of the Fae had last been seen in London.

"A year later, the Fae ambassador appeared at court, carrying a swaddled bundle. The king and queen of the Seelie court, on learning of the princess's condition, had delivered an ultimatum—either she left their realm, or the child did. The child, named Arwyn Fitzfey, was delivered to his human father to be raised. We can only imagine the toll borne by his mother, to give up her child and never see him again." Lady Loburn paced before the fireplace, her attention fixed on the carpet beneath her feet.

"The mad king has a half-Fae son?" Hannah gasped at the implications. "Why is this not widely known?" She leaned forward in her seat at the incredible news. Then her mind whirled, wondering if there were any paintings of the man. It was said that the Fae were so beautiful that it hurt human eyes to look upon them, hence they always wore hoods and veils when on English soil. But what of a half-Fae? He would be a stunning specimen.

"Shush, Hannah. Kitty will explain if you give her a chance." Seraphina raised a finger to her lips.

"Arwyn grew into a most handsome man, as you may expect, Hannah. He was much about court when Sera and I were navigating those waters in the 1780s and '90s. He had a gentle heart and often came to our rescue when the older nobles tried to cut us down. He wished people to live peacefully with one another. Perhaps swayed by his beauty and kindness, King George favoured him, and allowed him to sit in on many council meetings. There were rumours that the king sought a way to change the succession, arguing that a child of such royalty, with a foot in both king-doms, took precedence over his entirely human offspring, legitimate or not."

"I suspect that was not well received by the Prince Regent, his half-brother," Wycliff commented.

"No. It was not. Or by a particular coterie, led by the Duke of Harden, who argued long and hard that Arwyn should be excluded from both council and court. A vocal group of nobles held that a half-Fae had no right to interfere in either British politics or the succession. Remember, this was before the Unnaturals Act of 1813 and such creatures were still considered less than human. That prejudice extended to the Fae." Kitty stopped pacing and seated herself in the wing chair.

"What happened to Arwyn?" Hannah glanced from Lady Loburn to her mother. She wracked her brain but had never heard of the man, which meant history had erased his life. Why?

"The French revolution of 1789 set nobles and landowners on edge. They feared an uprising on English soil and agitated in Parliament for harsher measures to control the working class. Arwyn argued the opposite. He believed universal suffrage for men would defuse any revolutionary feelings. He thought governance should be spread to all the people. At the time, it appeared that George was listening to him, and favoured such a course." Lady Loburn took Seraphina's gloved hand in her own and seemed to draw strength from their long friendship.

Wycliff let out a low whistle. "That would have set most of the nobles against him."

Lady Loburn nodded. "Indeed. Men of privilege do not easily release their grip on power. The situation exploded when Arwyn argued that Napoleon was doing much good in Europe and that England should adopt some of his ideas. That was when the duke and his supporters decided to put an end to the *French Fae*, as they took to calling him."

"Who supported the duke? Although I suspect I will know their names." Wycliff hooked one ankle over his knee and rested his hands on his boot.

"The Viscounts Burroughs and Enderley, the Earl of Stoneleigh, and Baron Thornton. All led by the Duke of Harden." Kitty spat out the names as though they were bitter on her tongue.

"I assume they had Arwyn done away with, to end his influence over the king?" Wycliff asked.

Lady Loburn bowed her head and clasped Seraphina's hand tighter. Then she straightened her spine before continuing. "Harden agreed to a meeting in a picturesque cottage that Arwyn owned by a river. The duke said he wanted privacy to discuss the proposed legislation to give all men the vote. I tried to warn Arwyn, and pleaded with him not to meet the duke alone. But his generous heart could not imagine the other man harboured evil intent. In that little cottage, Arwyn was murdered and the house burned to the ground so that no trace of him remained."

Silence fell over the room. Hannah's heart ached for the man who wanted only a peaceful life for everyone. What a horrible way to die. Her father said that burns were the most painful type of injury.

Burns.

An idea sparked in her mind.

Wycliff dropped his foot to the ground and leaned one arm on his knee. "Of the men involved in that conspiracy, two of their sons are dead, and a third nearly died. Someone is targeting the sons for the sins of their fathers. Which means either Harden or Thornton is next."

"We need only determine who has taken up the flaming sword of justice after so many years," Seraphina said.

"Arwyn did not deserve such a death. Nor did his little son." Lady Loburn faced Hannah with unshed tears shimmering in her eyes.

"He had a son?" Hannah exclaimed.

"Yes. A lovely wee boy—Tristan. His mother had died in childbirth and Arwyn doted on him. Tristan had been with Arwyn that week at the cottage and would have been asleep in the house. We can only pray that he never woke when the fire consumed the structure." Lizzie's mother pulled a handkerchief from her reticule and dabbed at her eyes.

"Do you know positively that he died?" The idea became a certainty in Hannah's mind.

Lady Loburn froze, the handkerchief in mid-dab. "We never found his body, but he was only eight at the time and the fire so fierce."

"But you found Arwyn?" Wycliff leaned forward now, a bright light in his eyes.

"Yes. Or what remained of him. He was interred in a private ceremony and I think the grief is what created the fracture in King George's mind. He has not been sane since his beautiful boy was taken from us." She finished wiping her eyes and returned the handkerchief to her reticule.

Wycliff jumped to his feet. "Can you describe Arwyn's son?"

"Tristan favoured his mother, but enhanced with Arwyn's Fae beauty. He had dark hair and the most arresting blue eyes," Lady Loburn said.

"Baron Medwin has such colouring and suffered extensive burns some years ago," Hannah said. "The wronged son is delivering his vengeance on the sons of those who conspired to kill his father."

"But he is no vampyre." Wycliff leaned on the mantel and drummed his fingers against the marble.

While Wycliff pondered the finer details of the murders, a very different point gnawed at Hannah: Lady Loburn's deep sorrow at the narration of the unknown man's death. Why did the loss of a friend affect her so? Was there something more to this story? "Are there any pictures of Arwyn?"

"I possess a miniature." Lady Loburn pulled a small object from her reticule and handed it to Hannah. Rather than being the expected portrait in a frame, it was a locket. The engraving on the surface had worn smooth and was only visible in snatches, as though fingers had rubbed it constantly. Flicking the catch, Hannah prised the sides apart. Inside was the tiny visage of a very handsome man. Blond curls brushed his high cheekbones. Under perfectly arched eyebrows, eyes the colour of a clear blue summer's sky regarded the viewer. Lush, dark pink lips formed the perfect pout.

"I see why he was called Arwyn—the Welsh for *handsome*. There is something familiar in his gaze and appearance. The colouring and shape remind me of the angelic face of—" She glanced up as Lady Loburn closed her eyes. "Lizzie."

A lump wedged in Hannah's throat and she could say no more. She snapped the locket shut and handed it back to Lady Loburn. Her gaze darted to her mother as a horrible and unworthy thought grew in her mind. Impossible. Or was it? She had often pondered how Lizzie could possess such angelic beauty and bear no physical resemblance to either of her parents.

"Yes, to answer your question before you give it voice. I trust in your discretion." Lady Loburn met Hannah's wide-eyed stare. "I am fortunate that the marquess displayed his kind heart when my situation became known to him."

"Does she know?" A whirlwind of thoughts and emotions tore through Hannah's mind.

"No. In every way but one, the marquess is her father." Steel crept into Lady Loburn's tone.

Hannah had always considered Lizzie part angel. Now she'd learned that royal Fae blood flowed through her friend's veins and gifted her with otherworldly beauty. Lizzie was doubly royal—on her father's side was King George, her unacknowledged grandfather, and a Fae princess as her grandmother.

Then another thought seeped like a chill through her mind. Every day, Lady Loburn had to smile and let Harden into their house, knowing his father's envy had resulted in the death of her daughter's father. Her child would soon carry a name soaked in blood. The wound reopened over and over for decades to come.

Tears burned in Hannah's eyes and her breath came short in her chest. "What must it cost you, for Harden to marry Lizzie? For your future grandchildren to bear the name that caused you such grief?"

Lady Loburn moved to sit next to Hannah and took her hands. "Francis is a good man. I can categorically say he in no way resembles his father due to his most formidable mother. I will not lie—it pained me when he first courted Lizzie. But I watched him, and I have judged him on his actions and his own merits. Now I see the irony—the name of the man who tried to eradicate a bloodline from our court will offer that same bloodline protection and allow it to flourish."

Hannah tightened her grip on Lady Loburn's hands. She could not imagine the depths of the woman's forgiveness, to let her only child become part of a family she must hate. "We must find Baron Medwin and protect Harden. Lizzie would be devastated if anything happened to him."

Lady Loburn stroked Hannah's cheek and then nodded. "I will protect my child from experiencing the agony of losing the man she loves. Francis is a good man and should not be made to pay for the cowardly actions of his father."

"What happened to the late duke?" Hannah recalled that Francis had come into his title at a very young age. Possibly about the same time Arwyn was murdered. She cast a sharp glance to her mother. Seraphina had, on occasion, used her magic to deliver justice where the legal system failed, or was unable, to act.

"The duke died of a rather horrible and lingering ailment, not long after we buried Arwyn," Seraphina said.

"How coincidental. The others are lucky they did not suffer a similar contagion," Wycliff murmured.

"Yes. Weren't they?" The veil concealed her mother's face, but Hannah could hear the challenge in her words. "There is another reason why we must protect Lizzie. Her father and half-brother were to be slain to eradicate their bloodline, for the old duke knew Tristan slept upstairs that night. Powerful men feared that the descendants of King George and Deryn, who is now the Fae queen, might seize the crown. They do not know Lizzie is the last such descendant."

"We still haven't answered the question of *how* Medwin is killing the sons of the original five. We only know of one vampyre in London, and his bite does not correspond to the wounds inflicted on any of the men." Wycliff steered the conversation back to the more pressing concern. "Unless you think he sends out his little puppets to scurry around and do his bidding," he added with a sardonic huff.

Seraphina's head whipped around to Wycliff and electricity crackled in the air as she threw up her hands. "The puppets? Oh, my goodness. Of course—Hannah, we have been blind! They are not puppets! *They are fusil dryads.*"

"Fusil dryads? You think he has one doing his bidding?" Hannah picked the name from her memory and constructed an image to accompany what she knew. Dryads were woodland nymphs, normally only found in forests. Surely a creature that had stepped from an oak tree would cause a stir if it were seen in London?

"Not one, Hannah, six. They have a diminutive form as well as a more human-sized one." Her mother waved her hands and a creature shimmered before her the size of a pixie. Or a puppet.

Hannah jumped to her feet and rushed to a shelf. She plucked the book on the Fae from its place at eye level, and flicked through the pages to find the relevant passage. It was a scant two paragraphs with no illustrations. From the description, she had—erroneously, it transpired—assumed they were the Fae version of a vampyre.

The vision the mage created morphed and the creature snarled and bared its teeth. "Our eyes see wooden puppets and so our brains are closed to other possibilities. I never even considered them, because they are a creation of the Fae realm and have never crossed our threshold. They also—"

"—only obey the commands of Fae royalty," Hannah finished as she read from the book. "Baron Medwin has the blood of Fae royalty in his veins."

Hannah met Wycliff's gaze. One black eyebrow arched and he asked, "What, exactly, is a fusil dryad?"

She tapped the book and handed it over to Wycliff. "A blood pixie. Wooden creatures who sup on blood. Given the size of the *puppets* in the baron's possession, I would estimate each has a body of approximately the volume of a pint."

"Six pints would drain a man well beyond the point of death," Sir Hugh put in.

"The dolls are tiny enough to slip into a man's home without being noticed. They could climb up drainpipes and look like squirrels. No one would pay any heed to something so small." Hannah imagined one scaling the side of a house and squeezing into a bedroom through a window.

"They also sing, do they not?" Seraphina asked.

Hannah remembered the beautiful things strolling in the billiards-table garden. "When Baron Medwin conversed with them, it made me think of birdsong."

Wycliff snapped the book shut and dropped it on a side table. "They sing lullabies that pull the listener into a kind of stupor or trance. That would be the perfect opportunity to drain their blood. It also explains why Lord Enderley could not recall anything."

Excitement burned in Sir Hugh's eyes. "How do these pixie-sized vampyres work, my girl? Surely they would have tiny teeth?"

"The sucker is in their palm. It reveals itself when they press their hands to the victim," Seraphina said.

"Which would explain the slightly different bite marks. They weren't bites made with fangs at all, but the distance between doll-sized hands." Sir Hugh scratched his chin and his eyes rolled up to the ceiling in thought.

"Then the next doll used the same puncture wounds, to make it look as though a vampyre had drained the victim," Wycliff added.

"Tristan has been to the Fae realm." Seraphina turned to Lady Loburn. "Perhaps that explains why we found no trace of his body, Kitty? One can only wonder at the welcome the long-lost grandson would have encountered in their court, burned and suffering as he was. Or perhaps a watching agent of the Fae took him there to heal."

"Do you think his grandmother, Queen Deryn,

gave him these blood dolls with which to exact his revenge?" Lady Loburn asked.

"Let's seize him and his minions first. We can ask about family reunions later." Wycliff paced and rubbed one hand over the back of his neck. "We need to catch him in the act, for conclusive proof against him. If we can secure Thornton, I suggest we set a trap using Harden."

22

With her story told and no further assistance to offer, Lady Loburn took her leave to return to London.

Wycliff leaned on the fire surround and stared at the tiles as he considered what he would do if he were a crazed-and-crisped part-Fae. "I doubt these dolls roam the streets on their own, and they are too small to travel long distances. Medwin will use his carriage to get them as close to his victim as he dares. We need to ensure that if he goes to Thornton's house first, he will be dissuaded from releasing them and so will try Harden instead."

Seraphina wheeled herself to the middle of the room. "Hugh has experience in activating protection wards. I can create one that he can use to ensure Thornton is safe. I will add an extra element to make the house loud and light filled, as though he hosts a well-attended party. That should be sufficient to convince Medwin to try another night, and you can lay a trap at Harden's house."

"How do we catch these dolls? They are small and move fast." Wycliff conjured in his mind a farcical situation as they all dived after the darting creatures. Their size would work to their advantage and they might hide in places a human couldn't access. As the hound, he could incinerate them on the spot, but Harden might not appreciate his setting fire to the mansion, even if parts of it did need redecorating.

"Oh, Mother!" Hannah jumped to her feet and rushed to her mother's side. "What of the spell you cast over the chickens? The one that slows them down as though they walk through honey. That might work on the fusil dryads, as they are of a similar size."

The mage tilted her head as she considered the spell. "Yes, I believe it would. I can modify it so it is dispersed through the air, but only affects small things. We wouldn't want you or Wycliff slowed down as well. If I attach the spell to one of Percy's feathers, you can release it when the dolls enter the room."

"That would be most useful. Could you have both enchantments ready before dusk?" Wycliff asked.

The linen veil swayed as she nodded. "Yes, if I begin at once."

"I'll see you upstairs," Sir Hugh said, taking charge of the bathchair and steering his wife toward the door.

That solved one part of the problem, but he still didn't have enough men at his disposal to do all the tasks he needed this night. Wycliff paced, his hand curled into a fist. His blood heated at the prospect of throwing Hannah into danger yet again. "There are not enough of us. We need to be with Harden inside his home and outside to hunt Medwin."

Hannah watched her parents leave the room. "The easiest way is to split up. I will take the honey spell and go to Harden, and you must search for the baron. Might I suggest you take Frank?"

He had wondered about the giant man. While he moved slowly, as though under a permanent honey spell, he might be handy in a fight. "But that leaves you with no support."

"I will not be alone. I am given to understand from Lizzie that Harden is rather a sporting man. But I do have another idea if you would consider it. What of Sir Ewan? I cannot imagine anyone better to assist and if Lady Alice is willing, she may be able to locate the baron."

Being able to pinpoint the man's exact position would be handy and save Wycliff from roaming the streets flinging open carriage doors to peer inside. "But her gift requires something of Medwin's in order to locate him."

A quiet smile caressed Hannah's face. "Remember when we visited and I sneezed? He gave me his hand-kerchief. I still have it and it has not yet been laundered."

He stared at her, still amazed that he was blessed with a clever wife. The pieces fell into place in his mind. "Very well. I will take my horse, ride directly to

Shaw, and seek his assistance and his wife's. You take the carriage with your father and Frank. Sir Hugh can use the protective ward with Thornton and you can carry on to Harden's. You, Shaw, and Harden can lay in wait for these fusil dryads and I will use Lady Alice's help, if she is willing, to track down Medwin."

Wycliff rode for London and the town house occupied by Sir Ewan Shaw and his wife. He rapped on the door and hadn't cooled his heels for long before the door opened.

"Sir Ewan will see you, Lord Wycliff," the man intoned before Wycliff could open his mouth, and gestured for him to enter.

Wycliff handed off his top hat and gloves. It came as no surprise that the king's spymaster knew who knocked at his door. He was shown through to a modest study with a window that afforded a good view of who approached from the street.

The wolf sat on the edge of his desk, arms crossed over his chest, waiting. "What brings you to my door, Lord Wycliff—Ministry woes, or marital?"

Wycliff wondered if the man gathered far too many secrets and knew a little too much. But now was not the time to seek his confidence in how to tread delicately with Hannah. "Ministry. It transpires that our vampyre is no vampyre at all, but six little blood-drinking puppets."

One elegant eyebrow shot up. He pushed off the desk and gestured to the soft leather armchairs. "You will have to educate me in how exactly puppets drink blood."

Wycliff sat, but perched on the edge of the seat with one arm leaning on the side as he spoke. "These are not exactly puppets, but a Fae creature called a fusil dryad, or a blood nymph. Lady Miles says they are like wooden pixie vampyres. Baron Medwin has half a dozen of the things, and he is using them to kill certain men."

Shaw leaned back, elegantly crossing his legs at the knee. "Have you ascertained why he would do such a thing?"

"Revenge. He is visiting the sins of the fathers upon the sons." There was no justice in murdering men because of the actions their fathers had taken. Medwin should have gone to the king directly and sought action against the surviving men who had orchestrated Arwyn's death.

"You do need to stop speaking in riddles, my lord. Which sins of their fathers are the murdered men paying for?" Shaw rested his chin on his knuckle and eerie blue eyes regarded Wycliff.

Meeting the lycanthrope's predatory gaze made the hound surge over Wycliff in response, but he ordered it down. Now was not the time. "Over twenty years ago, Baron Medwin's father, Arwyn Fitzfey, was murdered in a plot constructed by the Duke of Harden, the Viscounts Burroughs and Enderley, the Earl of Stoneleigh, and Baron Thornton."

That broke through the serene mask Shaw wore.

Interest flared in his eyes and he leaned forward. "He survived the fire, then. I discovered a single account from a mad old woman who said fairies had spirited the boy away and that's why his body was never found."

"She most likely spoke the truth. Medwin had to have been in the Fae realm to possess the dryads. But how do you know of it?" The man opposite him was too young to have remembered the scandal of the half-Fae royal bastard. Wycliff himself had had no inkling until this evening. His father had never mentioned it, and yet it must have happened while he was still in favour at court.

Full lips quirked in a smile. "I am England's spymaster and it behooves me to know all about the king, to better predict any threats against him or the Prince Regent. I would never have guessed at an affair with a Fae princess and a love child, if not for the encrypted notes left by my predecessors."

Wycliff grunted. As he suspected, the man held too many secrets to his chest. "Since Medwin failed in his attempt with Enderley, who is now under constant watch by a vigilant mother, he will seek out either Harden or Thornton. Lady Miles is crafting a protective ward for Thornton so that we can lay a trap at Harden's house. I came here to seek your assistance. I need to trap the dolls as they seek to drain Harden's blood, and find wherever the baron hides in the dark. I cannot be in two places at once, and would prefer not to leave Hannah with only the duke for protection."

Wycliff curled his hand into a fist. Hannah was

capable with her mother's spells for protection, but the hound snarled at the thought of her being beyond his help should anything go awry. Nor did she know how to handle a weapon, should the need arise.

Shaw nodded and rose gracefully to his feet. "Of course. I've not had a spot of sport for some time."

Wycliff stood and clasped his hands behind his back. "Could I further trouble you for Lady Shaw's unique assistance? Hannah has an item of the baron's and we were hoping your wife could locate him in order to narrow my search."

Shaw laughed as the two men walked back to the foyer. "Once I tell her my tale of a Fae bastard and blood-sucking puppets, I suspect she will insist on being included."

At that moment, his wife emerged from the end of the hall. A smile lit her eyes as she approached. "Lord Wycliff, how pleasant to have your company. Is Lady Wycliff with you?"

"Lady Shaw." He nodded to her. "Yes and no. She is not here, but awaits us elsewhere. I came to seek the assistance of yourself and your husband with a certain matter."

"Oh?" She stopped next to her husband; he wrapped an arm around her waist and pulled her close to kiss her cheek. Alice rested a hand over her husband's heart. The two had a warm and easy affection with each other that Wycliff both admired and aspired to find with Hannah.

Her warmth made him smile in return. "Our

mission involves the child of a Fae princess, if I could leave Shaw to fill you in on all the sordid details?"

Her eyes sparkled as she regarded her husband.

"We must depart for the Duke of Harden's home, Alice, where Lady Wycliff waits for us. I will tell you this fairy-tale and its murderous end on the way there," the lycanthrope said.

"Then I shall fetch my bonnet and pelisse immediately, so as not to detain you gentlemen." She caressed her husband's cheek, nodded to Wycliff, and hurried back along the hall.

"I will ride to Harden and apprise him of the situation, and meet you there," Wycliff said, and the two men parted company.

A short ride later, he dismounted at the duke's residence as a footman rushed out of the house to take the reins of the horse.

"Is the duke in?" he asked as he jumped to the ground.

"Yes, my lord," the footman replied.

"You may have her unsaddled. I shall be here awhile." Wycliff patted the mare's rump and then rushed up the stairs and through the door held open by the butler. "The duke, immediately," Wycliff said as he stepped inside.

The butler closed the door and walked with measured steps that he refused to hurry to the study where Wycliff had met the duke previously. Once he was announced, Wycliff waited until the doors closed before striding across the carpet toward Harden.

"Wycliff. This is unexpected," Harden said as he set down his pen.

He halted before the desk, littered with invoices and holding a large accounts ledger. "I believe there may be an attempt on your life this evening, and I intend to stop it."

Harden's blue eyes widened. "Good God. Is this related to the deaths of Stoneleigh and Burroughs? But why me? I have little to do with them."

"Before I start, Hannah will be here soon, as will Sir Ewan Shaw and Lady Alice." Wycliff walked over to the twin sofas upholstered in brocade as the duke moved around his desk.

"Be seated, Wycliff. I'll tell my man to show them through as soon as they arrive." Harden stuck his head out the study door and had a hushed conversation with the butler before returning. He took the sofa opposite Wycliff. "Now, what is this all about?"

Wycliff briefly told the duke of the king's half-Fae bastard, the plot to kill him, and the son seeking revenge.

Harden leaned back in his seat. "To think my father led a plot to have this man murdered, rather than finding common ground. I find myself rather agreeing with this Arwyn—more say from the people in the governance of England might lead to a better country for all of us."

"Baron Medwin failed to kill Enderley and we have protection in place around Thornton. I plan to use you in a trap, so we can capture these dolls in the act of doing their master's bidding." As Wycliff finished his tale, the others arrived.

"I believe you wish me to locate Baron Medwin, but do you have an item that belongs to him?" Alice asked.

Hannah pulled the soiled handkerchief from her reticule and held it out to the other woman. "Will this allow you to locate Baron Medwin? I have not touched it too much."

Alice took the crumpled piece of cambric and clasped it between her palms with her eyes closed. "Yes, this will work. I'll also require a map."

"I have one." Harden went to a cabinet and flung open the doors. From within, he extracted a rolled-up sheet of paper. He untied the ribbon and unrolled it on the table between the sofas.

Alice seated herself before the map. In one hand she clutched the handkerchief, her other hand rested lightly on the paper. She described slow circles until her finger dropped on one spot. "He's here. But I sense he is moving."

Wycliff drew a path from the street indicated back to the mansion. "That is within walking distance from here. I will take Frank. Lady Shaw, do you feel up to accompanying us, in case he moves in the dark and we miss him?"

A sweet smile crossed her lips and she glanced at her husband. "Of course."

Wycliff turned to the duke. "If you could instruct your staff to blow out the lights and go to bed. We need the house to slumber. I doubt Medwin will send the dryads in if every window blazes."

Harden issued instructions to his butler, who departed on silent feet to convey the command to the rest of the staff.

In the entranceway, Hannah handed a set of warded beeswax ear plugs to Harden and Sir Ewan, to protect them from being lulled to sleep by the dolls' song. Then Alice slipped her hand through Frank's monstrous arm; the patchwork creature towered over her.

Hannah held Wycliff's gaze for a moment, then she followed Harden up the stairs to his bedchamber.

Sir Ewan stepped to Wycliff's side. "No harm will come to your wife while she is under my watch," he murmured.

Wycliff let out a short huff of relief, then held out his hand. "Likewise."

The two men shook. "You would have made an interesting addition to the Highland Wolves had you been born Scottish." A curious glint lit Shaw's eyes as he turned to follow Wycliff's wife.

23

Hannah followed Harden up the stairs and along a hall. He pushed open panelled double doors and stood aside for her to enter his private bedchamber. As she stood on the threshold, she appreciated having Sir Ewan present. How unseemly to be alone with the duke in his bedroom. Even Lizzie had never set foot in this room.

Hannah took a cautious step forward and drank in her surroundings. Lizzie would bombard her with questions when she found out. A large four-poster bed stood against one wall. The dark barley-twist posts reached toward the ceiling and held aloft a canopy in hues of gold and brown with flecks of vibrant red.

A large fireplace to one side was flanked by a worn leather armchair and a loveseat covered in red velvet. A doorway across from the bed stood partially ajar, lending a glimpse of the dressing room and where the valet slept, so he remained close to his master. Tall windows faced the front and silk curtains in gold and red were tied back with tassels the size of Hannah's fist.

"What shall I do?" Harden asked as he stood in the middle of his room.

Sir Ewan joined them and walked a circuit of the bedchamber, looking behind furniture and twitching the curtains. "Everything needs to appear normal when the puppets creep in. We need you in bed, wearing your nightshirt. Lady Wycliff and I will conceal ourselves in the shadows."

Hannah looked away to hide a blush. Surely the duke wouldn't remove his clothing while she was in the room? From the corner of her eye, she saw him approach a folded screen painted with cranes fishing in shallow water, and she breathed a little easier.

"Might I suggest a chair in the corner, Lady Wycliff? We can place it in the shadows and drape a blanket over you." Sir Ewan pointed to a slender chair with a striped fabric that was pushed against the wall.

Harden changed into his nightgown and emerged wearing a velvet robe and matching slippers on his feet. They set to work securing the room to ensure that once their prey entered, they wouldn't be leaving again. Sir Ewan locked the doors and pocketed the key. Next, the fire was stoked, to create a deterrent to any wooden creature that tried to escape up the chimney. All the windows save one were closed and the latches turned tight. Then Hannah drew all the curtains, leaving only a slender gap over the window left slightly ajar.

"What will you do with them, once you catch them?" Harden asked.

"Good question. We need a solid container." Sir Ewan frowned and surveyed the room.

They settled on a solid timber blanket box with a sturdy latch. Hannah lifted out all the blankets and piled them in the bottom of an armoire. Sir Ewan and the duke moved the box so it sat at the end of the bed and closer to the centre of the room.

"Right then," Harden said and clapped his hands together.

He seemed nervous as he bounced on the balls of his feet, but then, he was bait in a trap. Hannah wondered if they should have had Doctor Husom waiting downstairs with his equipment, in case the fusil dryads latched on to the duke before they could stop them. However, one look at how Sir Ewan prowled the room with lupine grace reassured Hannah that the Fae creatures stood little chance of succeeding this night.

With everything in place, there was nothing more to do except wait. The duke climbed into bed and fussed with his pillows and blankets. Hannah went to her corner. Sir Ewan blew out all the lights, but left two ensorcelled glow lamps. One by the bed cast a soft yellow light over Harden. The other seemed to be left on the writing desk to one side, but its light made a golden path from window to bed for their prey to follow.

Hannah drew her feet up under her and held the silken envelope in one hand. Inside, the spell attached to Percy's feather wriggled and tingled against her palm. Silence fell over the room, broken only by the tick of the clock and the rustle of blankets as the duke shifted in bed. Sir Ewan became a statue by the curtain, his eyes an eerie silver in the moonlight.

She wondered how Wycliff fared in the streets as he sought and apprehended Baron Medwin. Imagining what happened outside evolved into scenarios where the baron had other Fae creatures or devices to call upon. She chided herself that her husband had his own secret to protect him, and could potentially incinerate anyone who tried to harm him. Assuming he could change into the hound fast enough. That left her contemplating the cruel irony of Tristan, burned so horribly as a child, then set alight by a hellhound.

Hannah shifted in the chair to relieve the ache in her buttocks, when Sir Ewan held a finger to his lips.

They were coming.

Her heart clenched and Hannah sucked in her lips to stop herself from breathing too loudly. A gentle breeze stirred the curtain and then a soft plop was followed by several more, like large raindrops hitting metal. Small shapes appeared in the soft glow of the lamp. The fusil dryads crept across the floor. They were all clad in dark coloured trousers and waistcoats. Even the two females mimicked male clothing, although their waistcoats were laced at the back like corsets to hug wooden curves. Their shirts had triangular sleeves that flared out around their wrists.

A male fusil dryad took the lead and gestured for

the others to follow him. As they approached the bed, a lyrical, soothing song rose from them. Even with warded plugs in her ears, Hannah wanted to close her eyes and listen to their music. Two of the male puppets clambered up on the bed and then helped the others. Soon, all six gathered around Harden's torso, three on each side.

Hannah's heart tightened in her chest as she waited for the signal from the lycanthrope. How far would he let them go before intervening? They had proven how the creatures were able to enter a house unnoticed and lull their victim into a trance with their song.

Sir Ewan placed one hand on the window and pushed it shut. Then he gestured to Hannah. It was time to take action. She pulled the peacock feather from the silk and stood. The puppets whirled as she approached and their birdsong turned into excited twittering.

Hannah flourished the feather, waving it back and forth as she murmured the release spell. Her mother's honey spell detached itself from the feather and flew through the air like dust motes on a draft. The puppets scattered but it didn't matter—the magic would find them. Gleaming motes danced around the room and multiplied until a shimmering blanket draped itself over everything.

Her outstretched arm was mottled with gold dust, but her form was too large for the spell to take effect. The puppets trilled to each other as they ran, but their legs slowed to a brisk walk.

Harden flung back the blankets and grabbed up his robe. Even in the pursuit of murderous puppets, he covered his body first. Then he snatched up the closest puppet, about to dive under his bed.

"I have one!" Then he cried out and dropped the creature. "Ouch!"

"Be careful. They can still attack us, even if they are slowed down by the spell. Seize them by their arms." Hannah lunged at one of the females, who hurried back to the window.

Her hand closed around the creature's waist. The puppet struck out and a palm no bigger than Hannah's thumbnail pressed against her knuckles. A sharp stab shot over her skin, but Hannah grabbed a miniature wrist and pulled it off. A single drop of blood welled up from the wound. As the creature flailed its arm, Hannah managed to secure the other wrist. Soon she had one tiny prisoner and took the dryad to its blanket box prison.

With one blood puppet secure, Hannah pulled out a handkerchief and dabbed at the blood on the back of her hand. She peered at the puncture wound. "They do look like the impression of a single vampyre fang."

Sir Ewan's eyes shimmered like moonlight as he stalked the tiny dryads. He grabbed one by the back of its waistcoat and held it up to his face. The creature trilled and called at him and then wooden brows pulled together. "You won't be putting us to sleep," he said. Then one more was deposited in the box.

By the time they had caught four, all three hunters

bore puncture wounds from the vicious creatures. A regular thumping came from the prisoners trapped in the blanket box.

"They are trying to escape," Harden said. The top rattled and bumped as the dryads tried to work free the latch.

"They will not get past us tonight." Sir Ewan scanned the room.

"We are missing two. One woman and one man." Hannah got down on her knees and peered under the bed, but found only a covered chamber pot.

Searching for the missing dryads was like trying to hunt out a broody chook. Instead of pulling apart shrubs and leaves, they searched bedding, behind furniture, and flicked out curtains.

"There! Atop the curtain." Sir Ewan spied a male walking along the curtain rod. He stood on a chair and snatched the creature down. "Careful with the box lid, Lady Wycliff—the others will try to escape," Sir Ewan said as he held the struggling puppet.

"What if we drape a blanket over it and hold the ends down, leaving only a gap to thrust the next prisoner through?" Hannah suggested.

The wolf nodded. She fetched a large blanket that draped the box to touch the floor. She knelt on the edge of the blanket, so a puppet couldn't wriggle past. Then the duke raised the lid and the spymaster thrust the puppet in. The latch was shoved home before an escape attempt could be made.

"That leaves one." Harden sucked a knuckle as he surveyed his bedroom.

Hannah stood still and hoped that movement would catch her eye. "Would she have made her way out a window?"

Sir Ewan's nostrils flared as though he scented something, and he stalked across the room. "Not a window, but she was thinking of another way to escape."

By the armoire stood a wicker basket for laundry. The wolf lifted the lid and shoved his hand in. He withdrew a shirt that struggled in his grasp.

"Oh, that was clever. The maid would have picked up that basket and never looked inside." The duke manned the box lid and Hannah held the blanket over the top as the last prisoner was inserted, then the latch was locked.

"Let us hope Lord Wycliff was likewise successful in his hunt," Sir Ewan murmured, pocketing the key.

Wycliff, Frank, and Lady Shaw walked through the moonless night. No one spoke—not that Frank indulged in conversation anyway. In many ways, he was the perfect bit of muscle to accompany Wycliff. Lady Alice pointed when they came to a crossroad. At times, she closed her eyes and gripped the handkerchief in her gloved hands.

After nearly an hour of circling the streets around

Mayfair, they turned into a narrow mews. A carriage stood in the dark lane between the grand houses. The only noise was the heavy breathing of the horses, and the occasional scrape of a shod hoof on cobbles as the matched pair waited.

Wycliff took his bearings. By his estimation, they had made a large loop and circled back to the rear of Harden's home.

"Please stay out of sight, Lady Shaw. Your husband would be most displeased if anything happened to you," Wycliff murmured.

She flashed him a smile and whispered, "I shall stay beside Frank. He is a rather effective wall to shelter behind."

He trod on light feet and approached the carriage. He signalled for Frank, with Lady Alice in his shadow, to stand on the other side. Then Wycliff grabbed the handle, opened the door, and climbed into the carriage. He took the seat opposite its silent occupant.

The scarred face of Medwin turned to him. "Do you require a ride somewhere, Lord Wycliff?"

Wycliff struggled to reconcile the disfigured creature across from him with the legendary beauty of the Fae. It took little imagination to see Lady Elizabeth Loburn at home in the Seelie court. Her half-brother wasn't fit to empty chamber pots. "Yes. Newgate Prison. Unless you would prefer the Repository of Forgotten Things?"

The injured eye rolled to one side while its unaffected companion widened. "I don't know what you mean. Now if you don't mind, I have an assignation with a *friend* and I don't want her to find you in my carriage."

"Six friends, don't you mean?" he murmured. When Medwin remained silent, Wycliff continued. "You had them murder Burroughs and Stoneleigh. You almost added Enderley, but we managed to save him. You will fail with Harden. Hannah will have captured your bloodthirsty puppets by now. The only question remaining is what to do with you?"

Liquid heat rolled through him as the hellhound struggled to break free. The air within the carriage shimmered as the void began to materialise to demand the worthless soul before him. But Wycliff held the beast back. The void would have to wait. He would finish his task in this realm before he invoked the other.

Medwin lunged for the door and pulled it open, only to find his way blocked by the hulking mass of Frank.

"Bad man. Stay put," Frank hissed. His yellow eyes glowed in the dim light.

Medwin tumbled back into the interior and scrabbled for the other door. Wycliff grabbed him by the collar of his jacket, hauled him back, and hit him in the jaw. It was near impossible to have a fist fight in a carriage. Wycliff had to hit the other man while perched on the edge of the seat.

"Get your hands off me! I am royal twice over. My grandfather is King George and my grandmother Queen Deryn of the Sidhe. I am a prince of this realm and the rightful heir." His nostrils flared and sparks flew in his good eye.

Wycliff shoved Medwin back into the seat and leaned into him. "No. You are the bastard son of a bastard, who let your anger fester inside you. You should have gone to King George. He would not have been unsympathetic and might have given you a remote cottage in the countryside. Instead you chose to become a true monster who murders innocent men."

Medwin slapped away Wycliff's hand and tried again for the door. Wycliff punched him in the side of the head and the part-Fae tumbled to the floor and landed on his bottom. He climbed to the seat and threw himself into a corner. "They are not innocent. Their fathers conspired to change the course of English history and deprive me of my father and the crown."

Delusional and disfigured. Wycliff snorted. King George had many mad fancies, and politicians were well versed in making sure his decrees quietly disappeared. Arwyn might have had royal blood in his veins, but he was born on the wrong side of the blanket. Illegitimacy was a sin more unforgivable than being half-Fae in a society that struggled to adapt to the creatures in their midst.

"You failed and will be held accountable for your crimes. But I am curious about one thing—how did your puppets know whom to target? Since the men all seemed to suffer a cold at some point, I assume you did something during one of your evenings." Wycliff leaned back on the seat but didn't drop his guard.

Medwin snorted and turned his head away, hiding the burned half in shadow. For a moment, Wycliff saw the handsome man he could have been.

"A special viewing is all it took. The dryads sang and would lull the man into a trance. Then they all had a taste, to know the scent of him. That enables them to find the right person, when they gain access to the man's home. You cannot hold me. My grandmother will ensure I am freed. She gave them to me, you know. She burns for vengeance for the son who was torn from her." Fire burned in the man, ignited inside him the night his father was slain.

"Your grandmother has to hear of this first. Your existence and Arwyn's life were quietly erased from our history. I have no doubt your physical form will likewise disappear." The Repository of Forgotten Things would have its first royal resident.

Once they reconvened at the duke's home, Wycliff and Sir Ewan took charge of the prisoner and the locked box with his diminutive accomplices. They were all delivered to the Repository and interred in a room with a pleasant pastoral view from a window barred with iron—to ensure its Fae captives didn't slip through.

As Wycliff suspected, Medwin's history was kept from both the newspapers and the king. The papers reported only that a rogue vampyre had been responsible, and the creature duly executed through the surgical removal of his liver.

Two DAYS LATER, on the evening before the wedding
of the season, Hannah changed into her nightgown in
Lizzie's bedchamber. The two women spread out blankets and fat cushions in front of the fire. The coals were
ensorcelled by Seraphina and the flames burned in
tones of pink and green (to complement the colours in
Lizzie's room) and cast a soft warmth, but they weren't
unpleasantly hot.

On a low table the maids set out platters of fruit,
cheeses, tiny bites of pastry filled with savoury fillings,
and marzipan treats. Another tray held a pitcher of
lemonade and a carafe of wine. Lady Loburn agreed
the occasion called for a small drink, but not so much as
to impede her daughter's clarity of mind for the
wedding.

The lights were doused and the room lit only by the
flickering pastel flames. Hannah tugged a cushion up
behind her to lounge against the side of a sofa, and then

spread a blanket over her knees. Lizzie poured two glasses of wine, which practically drained the tiny carafe, and handed one to Hannah.

"You must tell me about married life with the viscount. You have been rather silent on the subject, Hannah. Are you simply trying to preserve my modesty? When we return from our wedding tour, I will tell you all about my wedding night with Harden." Lizzie leaned against her friend as they stared at the magical flames.

Hannah took a large sip of wine and considered what to say. She was already keeping two secrets from the sister of her heart. She examined her friend's features with a new understanding. From her earliest memory she had imagined Lizzie blessed by fairies with her porcelain skin, golden hair, ruby lips, and clear blue eyes. Never could she have imagined that actual Fae blood, or that of the Fae queen, coursed through her friend's veins.

If Lizzie was only a quarter Fae, Hannah wondered that mere mortals could look upon a full-blooded Fae. To see such beauty would surely steal the breath from your lungs. No wonder they said to go about hooded when in the human realm. Otherwise, people would drop dead of admiration at their feet.

There were some secrets Hannah could never tell Lizzie. Her true parentage was one. To reveal that would cause too much pain, and put her friend's life at risk from the men who sought to stomp out that blood-line. As Hannah sipped her wine, she realised she could not stomach adding another secret to her hoard. Far easier to share her troubles with her friend and seek her counsel.

"Ours was not a love match like yours will be, Lizzie. We wed for convenience and, I am afraid, there is little to share." Her fingers clenched the stem of the crystal wine glass while her emotions rioted. Their marriage of convenience had morphed into something else. The kisses she shared with Wycliff made her long to know more. Yet he hesitated. Why? Did he not find her desirable?

"Oh." Lizzie's eager expression fell away. She hid her disappointment behind the glass as she sipped her wine. A frown marred her pale brow and she placed the wine on the table to take Hannah's hand. "When you announced that you would marry Wycliff, I was desperately worried for you, Hannah. He is such a frightening man. But I sense that perhaps your feelings toward one another have changed?"

Hannah grasped Lizzie's hands and sorted through all she wished to unburden on her friend. "When he made his offer, I agreed to a marriage of convenience, so that I might assist Wycliff in his investigations of Unnatural crimes. In return, he agreed to extend to me the protection of his name and body."

The very words made a shiver work over Hannah's skin. He had said he would protect her with his body beyond death, and the words whispered of a deeper meaning still beyond her comprehension.

"The time we spent alone at Lady Fanny Pennicott's house party enabled us to establish a friendship. I also admit that we have kissed, and it—I was—" Words failed her. To be in his arms made fire burn through her veins and her lips tingle at the memory.

A tinkling laugh emerged from Lizzie's throat as she finished Hannah's sentence for her. "You enjoyed it? Or you found the kiss so delicious that it made your toes curl?"

Hannah stared at her friend. "Yes. How did you know?"

A faraway look came over Lizzie's eyes. "The look on your face is exactly how I feel on the inside after Harden has kissed me."

"That Wycliff has kissed me gives me hope there is attraction between us. I would like to...explore that further. But he has not made any sign that he wishes to claim his marital rights." There was the nub of the problem. Wycliff was legally entitled to possess her body, so why didn't he claim her? She struggled to believe he didn't want to. Not for any great reason of vanity, but because of the honesty of his reaction when he'd taken her in his arms in the glade. The look in his eyes set fire to her more completely than his hellhound form could. What, then, made him part company with her on the stairs, and walk the other way along the corridor to his room?

"Have you considered the possibility that while you might be married, he may in fact be taking his time to woo you?" Lizzie turned to sit facing Hannah, with the pink and green flames a halo in her blonde hair from behind.

Hannah snorted. Wycliff—wooing her? The idea seemed ridiculous. "Why on earth would he do that?"

"Perhaps he has feelings for you, but wants to ensure they are returned before he sweeps you into the bedchamber. Not all men are brutes, Hannah. Some are rather fond of their wives." Lizzie nudged her elbow and Hannah raised the glass to her lips.

Could Wycliff truly be taking things slowly between them, to allow her to come to terms with the next logical step in their relationship?

"How did you become so all-knowing about such things?" Hannah narrowed her gaze at her friend. The intimate workings of marriage should never have been whispered within earshot of an unmarried young lady.

"I love Harden and tomorrow is our wedding day. Nothing was going to stop our being joined. Do you really think that for the last two years, I have existed on kisses alone?" Lizzie grinned and drank from her wine.

Hannah stared at her friend with her jaw hanging open. She was both scandalised and indignant that her friend had held so tightly on to that particular secret. "Lady Elizabeth Loburn...well, I never!"

THE WEDDING of Lady Elizabeth Loburn to Francis, Duke of Harden, took place in an intimate little stone church with only their closest friends and family present. Seraphina created a magical world inside the old building. Silver water flowed along the aisle and blush-pink swans glided upon it. Rose petals fell from the air to scatter about Lizzie as she kissed her father and walked forward alone to meet her groom.

Later, as they entered the ballroom, an ice dragon rose up from the floor. A fairy princess wielding a sword stood in the middle of the floor to do battle with the beast. The dragon slid along the floor, throwing up a shower of snow from his claws, and halted inches from the princess. Then he turned into a handsome ice prince who danced with the princess. At the end, both turned into smaller dragons who flew up and settled on a balcony to watch the proceedings below.

Later that night, as Wycliff prowled the hall outside the ballroom, Earl Stoneleigh approached him. The older man's jaw was set in a hard line and his gaze was chilly, like ice over a pond in the middle of winter. "Thank you for catching the man responsible for my son's death. I still cannot understand what creates such a monster."

Wycliff ground his teeth and cast around. A flash caught his eye. "I can answer that question for you." He gestured for the earl to follow him and they walked a little farther along the hall. "This is who created such a monster."

Stoneleigh stepped forward and then turned on Wycliff. "Do you think this is a joke? My son was murdered in his prime and you tell me to look in a mirror?"

Wycliff tucked his hands behind his back. "Your son was murdered by Tristan, son of Arwyn Fitzfey."

The earl sucked in a breath. "What? The newspapers reported that a rogue vampyre was the fiend."

"A convenient lie. But if you prefer, I can go the newspapers and give them the full and correct version. Then London, and the king, will know that you and your cohorts murdered Arwyn and then left his son, the king's grandson, to burn in his bed. I believe you told the king it had been a terrible accident that killed them both, did you not?" Wycliff had little sympathy for the man. His own actions and prejudices had created the monster who had lashed out twenty years later.

The earl turned bright red. His breath puffed in and out and his eyes showed their whites like a panicked horse. After a full minute, he regained control of his temper. "You know nothing of it," he hissed.

"I know you murdered a gentle soul and lied to the king. Or did you think such actions would have no consequences? Life has a strange way of evening the odds. Now, if you'll excuse me, I intend to enjoy this evening." Wycliff left the man to stew in his own vitriol. Stoneleigh hadn't deserved to die. Neither had Burroughs or Arwyn. Two wrongs didn't make a right.

Back in the ballroom, Wycliff took a glass of champagne and stood to one side, finding his wife out on the floor. Hannah laughed as she partnered the radiant bride in a country dance. Then a chill raised his hackles as though a winter breeze gusted through an open window. "Shaw," he said without turning to his companion.

"Lady Miles has created a truly memorable day for the happy couple." The lycanthrope gestured to the dragons on the balcony, who occasionally roared and spat either rose petals or glitter over the dancers below.

"Yes. But then, she is an extraordinary mage." His opinion of the dead mage had changed over time. Through the veil, he saw the woman who loved her family and who wielded her power to better the lives of everyone within her reach. Her daughter, while born without any magic, still had her own unique abilities.

"Her daughter is also an extraordinary woman. It is no easy thing for men like us to find a woman who is strong enough to love and recognise our souls, whatever form they take." Shaw turned to Wycliff and piercing blue eyes regarded him.

Wycliff swallowed. Did Hannah love him? He clutched his glass tighter as he considered the possibility. She might, or she might not. His wife treated all she encountered in a kind and gentle manner. That didn't mean she loved everyone. Yet again, when faced with a difficult choice, he found himself paralysed by fear. To ask the question of her ran the risk of having his heart carved out with a spoon.

"While we have a mutual regard for one another, our marriage was one of practicality. How..." Wycliff's words trailed away, the question unasked. *How does a man know if his wife loves him? Or if she does not, is it at all possible to foster a greater feeling of devotion?*

"If you cannot find the words to tell her how you feel, Wycliff, show her instead. Words alone are empty unless accompanied by actions. Wrap her in your devotion and your feelings will filter through to her." Shaw murmured his advice as his gaze found his wife and locked on to her form.

"Unless she does not reciprocate that feeling and my devotion slides away like water off a duck's feathers." The words were dry in his mouth and he took another sip to moisten his throat. Ironic that he had married out of honour, and while he offered his name and body in protection, now he wanted his wife to seek much more from him.

Shaw laughed. "I've seen the two of you together, and there is much that lies unspoken. From my observation, quiet women are like still waters. Many people will walk past and never realise how deep they go. Only a brave man can take the plunge and discover what they harbour in their depths."

In that moment, Wycliff decided to ask Hannah to go to Dorset with him. There, along the beaches he had loved as a child, he would find the bravery to discover how deep their affection for each other ran. He raised his glass to Shaw. "To still waters and hidden depths."

Seraphina sat in a quiet corner cast in the shadows of potted trees, and watched the celebrations. Kitty joined her, a glass of champagne in her hand. The old friends sat in silence for several long minutes.

"I think you are a genius among mages," Kitty said at length.

"Thank you, Kitty. You know I adore Lizzie, and wanted the most magical day for her." She was particularly proud of her ice princess, modelled on Queen Deryn, Lizzie's Fae grandmother. Not that anyone would ever know.

"I was referring to another enchantment. One that has its own mind and does not follow any magical directions." Kitty tipped her wine glass toward two particular dancers, dark heads bent together. Wycliff smiled at his wife and Hannah glowed under his regard.

"It is clear to any observer that there is genuine affection between Hannah and Wycliff. However did you know, when you asked me to include him on the guest list for the engagement ball?" Kitty asked.

"I didn't. There was a higher authority directing my hand." While he didn't possess a fortune and prickled like a hedgehog, Wycliff was a loyal hellhound who would protect her daughter both in this world and the next. That he appeared to genuinely love Hannah, delighted Seraphina. Even though the couple were still unaware of their true feelings for one another.

Kitty's eyes widened in surprise. *God?* she mouthed.

"Well, a god, I am sure, but not the Christian one." Seraphina huffed a small laugh. If the god responsible for guiding her hand revealed themselves to be who she suspected, they dwelt in rather the opposite direction.

"Whoever it was, I am glad that Hannah has found a spouse who looks at her in such an enamoured way. I have no doubt he will prove a loyal and protective husband, who will not abandon her when your magic fails." Kitty sipped her wine and glanced to her lifelong friend.

Seraphina smoothed the cream silk over her knees. There was no point in lying to Kitty. They had been friends for too many years. "How did you know?"

"We have never had secrets between us. While Hannah told Lizzie that she never opened the pot of infected face powder, I happen to know that was a lie. I saw Hannah powder her face with it that night, as she waited for your carriage."

"You never said anything."

Kitty took Seraphina's gloved hand in hers and patted it. "I know what lies in your heart. I am sure you and Hannah only wanted to protect Lizzie from the pain of knowing her gift will one day cause Hannah's death. But I wonder if we do Lizzie a disservice in protecting her. She is stronger than she appears. Sometimes it is only when a friendship is tested that you realise how strong it truly is."

Seraphina blew out a sigh and the muslin over her face puffed out. The veil cast her world in a dreamlike haze. They seemed no closer to a cure and with the death of Mage Dupré, it was possible they might never reverse the dark magic he'd cast. That made her weep at night. Not for herself, but for all that the curse stole from Hannah and the other young women Afflicted by it. But there was one option yet. A dark path the hell-hound could walk to the underworld.

"One day, we will tell Lizzie. But not today. We are ever hopeful of a cure. Will you tell her the truth of her heritage?" They had added another secret to the burden Hannah carried. Kitty was right. There shouldn't be secrets between such close friends.

Kitty glanced about before replying in a hushed tone, "There is nothing to be gained by telling her of Arwyn. The marquess is a devoted father and could not love her more if she were his own blood. I worry that telling Lizzie would alter their relationship, and I would not wish that pain upon Loburn. Besides, I would not have her become a target of any fanatics who want to erase all last traces of Arwyn. Let him remain locked in my heart alone."

Seraphina raised her empty glass. "To protecting our children."

She would find a cure for Hannah if she had to wrest it from the underworld with every scrap of magic at her disposal. A plan took form in her mind—one that involved confronting whatever lay at the end of a certain dark path.

She was already dead. What else could Hades, or Anubis, do to her?

HANNAH AND WYCLIFF continue their journey in:

SIXPENCE and SELKIES
Manners and Monsters book 5
A heart as lonely as the ocean...

Hannah and Wycliff arrive at his ancestral estate in Dorset as tragedy strikes the coastal village. A young woman has lost her life to the tempestuous ocean, but only Hannah suspects the woman's death is anything but a horrible accident. As Hannah learns more about life in the close-knit community, she discovers two other women lost their lives to the sea. Or did they?

A rift grows between the young couple, as Wycliff refuses to believe another hand was responsible for the deaths. With her husband consumed by the needs of the long neglected estate, Hannah is left to her own devices and finds herself walking the same lonely path as the dead women.

Can Hannah and Wycliff heal the chasm in their relationship, or will Hannah succumb to the call of the ocean...?

Did you enjoy VANITY and VAMPYRES?

Thanks so much for reading *Vanity and Vampyres* and I hope you enjoyed it.

Please consider taking a moment to share your thoughts by leaving a review at the retailer where you purchased this book. Reader reviews help other readers discover new books.

Thank you, Tilly

ABOUT THE AUTHOR

Tilly drinks entirely too much coffee, likes to watch Buffy the Vampire Slayer and wishes she could talk to Jane Austen. Sometimes she imagines a world where the Bennet sisters lived near the Hellmouth. Or that might be a fanciful imagining brought on by too much caffeine.

To be the first to hear about new releases and special offers sign up at:
www.tillywallace.com/newsletter

Tilly would love to hear from you:
www.tillywallace.com
tilly@tillywallace.com

facebook.com/tillywallaceauthor
bookbub.com/authors/tilly-wallace

Printed in Great Britain
by Amazon